Life
is a
Cabernet

VALERIE HIMICK

For my mother, who taught me to read and to love books.

For my husband, Brian, who inspires me everyday.

With huge thanks to my many friends and family who gave me support, encouragement, proofreading, ideas, and advice. A special thank you to Jim for reminding me of the difference between anxious and eager and his many other suggestions and corrections.

A toast to the winemakers of Grand Traverse and Leelanau Counties for your wonderful wines, many of which were consumed during the creation of this book.

Cheers!

Chloe Sparkles– A semi-sweet, sparkling wine with just the right touch of tartness and a hint of palest pink in the color. A surprise to all of the senses. A fresh bouquet of spring's early awakening buds with the earthiness of newly turned garden loam. Starts off soft and smooth, then explodes like a spring thunderstorm. The memory lingers long after the glass is drained. Always a winner in blind taste tests. Try it for a romantic dinner for that taste of spring in the dead of winter.

Chapter 1

SPARKS

Chloe

I never Google a guy before the first date. I think it's better to retain some mystery and get to know each other gradually. Romance and mystery go hand-in-hand in my book. There's excitement in learning new things about each other as your friendship and, hopefully, your passion grows into a beautiful relationship or fizzles and dies.

Where's the fun in a blind date if you already know all about the guy before you decide to accept? My friends want every detail of a guy's biography and physical traits before they will even consider accepting a blind date. I go into a blind date blindly. I know nothing about him except when and where to meet and he knows nothing about me except that I will be at the appointed place at the appointed time with some prearranged clue for him to find me. I'll be the girl waiting on the bench in front of the restaurant wearing an orange and purple striped hat or holding a copy of some obscure book for identification.

I learned the hard way that if I'm using a book, it has to be an obscure one. Once, when it was on all of the Best Seller lists, I used a copy of *Twilight* as my identification. I was waiting in a park, and waiting, and waiting, when I finally noticed that everyone there was reading *Twilight*. So much for that blind date. Some unsuspecting girl, quietly reading her book in the park, must have liked him enough to take my place. I hope they had fun! I imagine they fell madly in love and are now happily married, living in a little house by the sea with a white picket fence, 2.5 children, and a cat.

Once my blind date and I do connect, I still like to proceed slowly. Some guys can give you their whole life story over appetizers – where they were born, what their parents did for a living, the name of their first grade teacher, all the dogs and pals they had as kids, favorite sports teams, all the rock concerts ever attended, every vacation ever taken, every job ever held, best high school high jinks, favorite drink and how many times they've been drunk on it, and favorite color. Oh yes, and all their ex-girlfriends and what went wrong with every relationship. Then they grill me with questions to see if I might be anything like any of those ex-girlfriends. When a guy starts that routine, I break his heart quickly and refuse a second date. Why bother? I already know all there is to know about him by dessert and I'm not sticking around for a nightcap!

I don't do on-line matchmaking sites either. I want my first contact with a guy to be in person, not in cyberspace.

Oh, and have you heard about those speed dating marathons? A different man every five minutes giving you his life story and his best lines, then a bell rings and off he goes to the next girl at the next table for a repeat of the same story and lines. No thank you!

I've been working on my dating strategy for several years with limited success. Here are some examples -

Duncan - I met him in the park a couple of Julys ago. I was rollerblading and he was jogging. I took one look at him, lost my balance and, literally, fell at his feet. Tall, dark and handsome with beautiful blue eyes, a deadly combination. He picked me up, literally, dusted me off and bought me lunch at a hot dog cart. That was the start of a beautiful summer romance. We always met at the park, ate many hot dogs, and had deep discussions about anything but ourselves. I thought I'd found my soul mate - until the day his wife and daughter came to the park with him. I guess there are some things I really need to know about a guy before I get too carried away. Oh well, lesson learned. But not all of the good looking ones are married.

Ben – I met him on a blind date. My friend Robin arranged it. Robin is happily married to Gary, and Gary had a single coworker named Ben. That's all I knew about him, but that was enough, since I trusted Robin and Gary not to set me up with another married man. Ben and I met in an art museum. He knew me by the artsy printed scarf I wore. I knew him by his perfectly coifed blond hair and his beautifully cut sport coat. Robin had told me he was a very sharp dresser, but nothing else. Ben and I spent many enjoyable evenings going to art shows, the symphony, and foreign films. We discussed art, music and theater but nothing more personal until the evening he invited me to dinner in his apartment. I came prepared with a good bottle of wine and new Victoria's Secret underthings. That was the evening Ben and I revealed our true selves to each other. He's still one of my best friends and I like his partner, Dane, a lot too.

Luke – I met him on the beach. There I was, looking hot in my new black bikini and sunglasses, sipping pink lemonade and perusing the latest issue of *Car and Driver*, when this equally hot hunk stopped dead in his tracks, dropped down in the sand next to me and started chatting me up about classic cars. The next weekend we were off to Detroit and the Woodward Dream Cruise in his 1968 Corvette. That was a very hot weekend! But summer ended, the Corvette went into storage, and Luke was only lukewarm without it.

Alex – I met him on Mackinaw Island one June. There's the perfect spot for romance. Mackinaw Island in the spring smells of lilacs, fudge, and horse droppings. I should have googled Alex, I would have learned a lot. But Mackinaw Island prides itself on being historic. No cars, just horses and bikes. Not the kind of place with internet cafes on every corner. Have you seen the movie *Somewhere in Time,* the romantic time travel movie filmed on Mackinaw Island? Well, Alex looked like Christopher Reeve in that movie and made me feel as beautiful as Jane Seymour. Turned out that he was a very good actor and starring in a play. He was feeding me lines - from the script. Without a script, he couldn't carry on a conversation.

I've met guys in all sorts of places and all sorts of ways. The usual - school, work, library, parties, bars, friends of friends. The not so usual – in line at the grocery store check-out, at a movie during the Traverse City Film Fest, in the beer tent at the National Cherry Festival, and while floating down the Platte River on a hot sunny day.

I dated the cop who stopped me for running a red light, the Good Samaritan who helped me fix a flat tire on my bike, the guy I met while pumping gas, the electrician who came out to Northern Lights to fix the electrical problems in the old building, the cute techie at the cell phone store, the best man at my friend Mandy's wedding, and a few years later I dated a guy I met while waiting in line with Mandy and her son to see Santa. Single dad, nice guy, cute kid.

With one exception, that I don't want to go into here, they have all been nice guys and I had lots of fun, but not one of them swept me off my feet and fulfilled all my romantic fantasies. I guess I've always had this vision of a handsome stranger riding in on a white horse, slaying the evil dragon, and carrying me off to his castle. My hero! Where is he?

By now, you might wonder where this is heading. Do I have a story to tell here or am I just going to share my dating philosophy and bore you with tales of the guys who didn't work out? But that's just some background about me, so you can understand why, when I met Joe, things happened they way they did. It wasn't really my fault.

I suppose I should introduce myself. After all, this isn't a date and if I want you to stick around and read this whole story, you deserve to know a bit about who's telling it. My name is Chloe Applewhite. I'm 28 years old, five foot five inches tall and my weight is proportionate to my height, as they say in the singles ads. My mother says I'm beautiful.

I was born in Bay City, Michigan and my first grade teacher, in case you care, was Mrs. Smith. When I was growing up, we had many family vacations in northwest Michigan, near Traverse City. I fell in love with the lakes and hills in that area and when I was eighteen and graduated from Bay City Central High School, I decided to go to college in Traverse City at Northwestern Michigan College. I earned an associate's degree in Liberal Arts which made me well qualified for nothing specific. I found a great job in one of the local wineries. I pour wine for tourists and manage the tasting room and retail store at Northern Lights Winery. I've come to love the wine business and can't imagine ever working anywhere else.

Thanks to my dearly loved, generous Great Aunt Gertrude, who left me a bit of an inheritance, I was able to buy a small, two bedroom two bath condo near Grand Traverse Bay before real estate prices here went completely bonkers. My best friend, Lilianna Oberlin, shares it with me.

I think my life is perfect. Almost. All I need is to find Mr. Right. I have lots of friends and a pretty active social life but I want more. I want to be the most important person in the world to someone. Someone besides my mother that is.

Here's my story…

Nobody in Northern Michigan believes that February really is the shortest month of the year. It's cold and it's dark. The fun of Christmas and New Years is a faded memory and spring is a distant dream. February is especially dreary when you're facing Valentine's Day without a boyfriend. Everything is hearts and flowers and diamonds and chocolates and new perfume and sexy lingerie and I was feeling very lonely.

"I guess it's just you and me, old girl," I said to Coco, the Northern Lights wine dog. She was sleeping on the rug by the fireplace and only twitched an ear to show that she heard me. Coco is a six year old brown and white Border Collie mix and a very good listener.

Then Joe walked into the Northern Lights tasting room. I noticed him right away. It was hard not to, he was the only customer that cold, gray afternoon. About six feet tall, good build, dark hair slightly curling with dampness as he pulled off his ski cap and approached the wine bar. My radar went into high gear. Around my age, I guessed, maybe 30, and as he removed his gloves, I discreetly checked out his left hand. Good, no ring. And he was very nice looking. Somewhere between movie-star handsome and boy-next-door cute.

Coco, who usually ignored the customers unless they made a fuss over her, jumped up from the rug and eagerly trotted straight to him. She was licking his hands and generally making a fool of herself over him. To tell the truth, I kind of felt like doing the same thing.

"Hello", I smiled at him, tucking the Vogue magazine that I'd been dreamily leafing through under the counter. "Welcome to Northern

Lights. Come on in and get warm. There's plenty of room by the fireplace today. What can I get for you?"

"Actually," he replied, "I'm not here for the wine. I'm here to see Tommy. Is he in?"

Tommy North is the owner of Northern Lights and my boss. "I'm sorry," I answered. "It was so slow here today that Tommy left to run a few errands, but he should be back soon. If you'd like to wait you can try some wine. I'll bet I can make a wine lover out of you by the time Tommy walks in."

He eyed me speculatively and I found myself blushing under his gaze - the curse of fair-skinned blonds like myself. "Do you have a preference for reds or whites? Sweet or dry? Or maybe sparkling wine? We have a wonderful selection here. The sparkling is my favorite. In fact, Tommy named my favorite after me. It's called *Chloe Sparkles*. I'm Chloe." I was now babbling and blushing. "Make yourself comfortable by the fireplace, you look like you're half frozen, and I'll bring a selection over to you. It's much warmer there than at the bar. There seems to be a draft in here today. Is it very windy outside? The weather seems to have kept all of our customers away today."

He hesitated for a moment then said "Thanks, that will be nice. I am a bit thirsty. It's nice to meet you, Chloe. I'm Joe." He sat down in one of the old leather club chairs we kept drawn up by the big stone fireplace, Coco sat at his feet with her head in his lap.

When Tommy and his wife, Jillian, opened Northern Lights, they converted an old horse stable on the property into the tasting room and offices. They added the big stone fireplace and modern plumbing. They cleaned, insulated, rewired, reroofed, and made the place cozy and charming, if still a little drafty on windy winter days.

Behind the bar, I quickly assembled the tray we used for fireplace tastings. Our dry reisling, chardonny, and gewurztraminer to start. The reds next, cabernet, merlot, and pinot noir. Then the *Chloe Sparkles* and to finish, our special cherry port. I added an assortment of wine glasses and some crackers and cheese to cleanse the palate between tastings, and some chocolate kisses to have with the cherry port.

I sat in the other chair and put the tray down of the table between us. "We start with Blue Moon, our reisling. Most reisling comes from Germany, but the growers here have found that our climate is perfect for it. It's an early ripening grape that does very well in northern Michigan. Reisling wines tend to be sweet, but here at Northern Lights, Tommy makes a great dry reisling with very little residual sugar in the wine." I poured a small amount from the blue bottle into the glass and handed it to Joe."

"Why is it in a blue bottle?" he asked.

"Just traditional with reislings. It doesn't affect the taste, but it looks nice."

He took the glass from me, sniffed the wine, and took a small sip. His eyes lit up and he looked at me with a surprised smile. "Not at all what I expected," he said. "It tastes like green apples…no pears…green grapes…and something else kind of lemony, but not lemons."

"Very good!" I told him. "It's a mineral taste."

"Like sucking on stones," Joe said. "But in a good way."

I laughed. "I've never heard it described that way before. Glad you like it. Ready for the next?"

Joe nodded and held out his glass.

"Chardonnay is a very versatile grape, it's fairly easy to grow just about anywhere in the world and it makes great wine in a variety of styles. Northern Lights Chardonnay is made in the traditional style and aged in French oak barrels." I poured the golden wine into Joe's glass.

"I can see the difference in color from the reisling. Even though they are both white wines, this one is darker, more yellow, almost honey colored."

"We call it Bottled Sunshine. The color reminds me of the late afternoon sun in summertime. Go ahead and try it." I watched him take a sip, then another.

"Ummm…it looks like honey but tastes more like fruit with butter or cream, or butterscotch. That's what it is – butterscotch. Remember that old Joni Mitchell song – *And the sun poured in like butterscotch and stuck to all my senses*?"

We finished singing together. *"Won't you stay, we'll put on the day, and we'll talk in present tenses.* I love it! *Chelsea Morning*! Perfect! I wonder if we can change the name."

Wow, a cute guy who knows oldies!

"Have a couple of crackers before you taste the next one," I said as I handed him the plate. "It will cleanse your palate so you get the full effect of gewürztraminer. I think you'll really like this one."

Joe smiled, "I've liked them all so far. What's this one called?"

"Sugar and Spice," I answered as I poured for him. It's semi-dry. In wine speak, dry means not sweet. So this one has a bit more sugar than the reisling or chardonnay you just tried."

I watched for his reaction as he took a sip, then another.

"Fruit and cloves and flowers, I think."

"You are good at this. Most first time tasters don't get all the subtleties of flavor."

Joe seemed uncomfortable with the compliment and quickly asked, "What would you serve with this wine?"

"It's perfect with Thanksgiving dinner, turkey and sage stuffing, but if you don't want to wait till November, try it with spicy Asian or Indian food."

"Yum!" Joe smacked his lips and finished the wine in his glass before holding it out to me. "Please miss, may I have some more?"

I laughed, "More of this or are you ready to move onto the reds?"

"Both!" he replied and I poured another little splash of Sugar and Spice for him then got clean glasses and turned to the reds.

"This is our award winning blend of Cabernet Franc and Merlot." I poured and handed the glass to Joe. He held it up and studied the color by the light of the fire.

"Beautiful," he said softly, smiling at me. "What would you call this color?"

I picked up the bottle and showed him the label. "Tommy calls it Ruby Lips." On the label was a life size, lipsticked, full-puckered lip impression.

"Yours?" Joe asked, one brow raised quizzically, very cutely I thought. Was he looking at my lips?

"Jillian's. Tommy's wife." I poured myself a taste and sipped.

"Oh, yeah. Ruby Lips." Joe was definitely looking at my lips now.

I held my glass up to the fire as he had done. It is a beautiful color. I love red. Joe must have been reading my mind. "What's your favorite red thing, besides wine – and rubies?" he asked me.

"Raspberries!" I replied.

"Fire Engines!" he countered.

"Cherries"

"Barns"

"Cashmere sweaters"

"Red licorice"

"Candy Apples"

"A '67 Corvette in Candy Apple Red!"

"A red velvet heart shaped box with a red satin ribbon filled with chocolate."

"Geraniums"

"Roses"

"Oh, yeah," Joe said. "Rubies and roses and red velvet boxes. Red - the color of love and romance. I still like the Corvette best."

"Do you have one?" I asked, hoping Joe wasn't another car guy like Luke.

"Not yet, someday maybe." He finished off his glass of Ruby Lips and reached out to the tray for a cracker. "What's next?" His lips were stained ruby. I tore my gaze away and picked up the Cabernet and poured us each a generous taste.

"To life!" I said raising my glass to his.

Joe looked confused. "Life," I explained, "Is the name of our Cabernet wine."

"I get it! Life is a Cabernet! Very good, and so is the wine."

I moved on to the next bottle. "This is Aurora, our Pinot Noir. Tommy named it after his mother. Aurora Borealis is the Latin name for the Northern Lights. Tommy wanted to call it Boring Alice, but Aurora put her foot down."

"This is a terrific wine", Joe said appreciatively, again holding up the glass and eying the color.

"The Grand Traverse region is especially known for its reislings, but our cool climate and the proximity to Lake Michigan make this region perfect for growing the pinot grapes, also. I think it's the best place in Michigan to live too. I moved up here about 10 years ago from Bay City." Okay, this was his opening to tell me where he was from. Instead he held out his glass to me.

"One more taste of this one please", he asked. I poured and watched as he twirled the wine in his glass and checked for legs. He lifted the glass to his nose and inhaled deeply, eyes closed in concentration. He took a good mouthful and held it, letting the flavor develop in the warmth of his mouth. He's no wine novice, I thought. He knows what he's doing.

"Ummmm – this is what roses taste like. What would you serve with this?" he asked me. "I can imagine it with just about anything, from venison stew to chicken salad sandwiches."

"You're right. It's a great all purpose red. I like it with salads, ribs, burgers, even hot dogs, with chili sauce, of course."

"Of course. But it has to be Motown style, no beans in the chili sauce, with onions and mustard."

I laughed. "You're making me hungry. I haven't had a good chili dog since last summer."

Joe reached for the tray again and spread some cheese over a cracker. "How about a cracker instead? It's all I can offer you right now." Our fingers touched briefly as I took the cracker from him.

We laughed, nibbled on cheese and crackers, and kept on sampling the various wines as the snow continued to fall and the afternoon deepened into evening. When the fire burned low, Joe added a few more logs from the wood rack to keep it burning. I don't usually drink with the customers, but that afternoon, I almost forgot that I was working. I kept the wine flowing, but my usual sales talk vanished and we were soon chatting like old friends – except Joe never told me one thing about himself.

We were down to the last two bottles on the tray. "Now for my favorite, but this bottle has been out of the fridge for too long. Let me get a colder one." I took the bottle of Chloe Sparkles back to the bar and replaced it with one from the refrigerator.

KIMBALL MIDWEST

COLUMBUS, OH
(800) 233-1294

NAVISTAR
877 332 9239
705565
M38

"With a cold bottle, the cork is easier to remove and it's less likely that the wine will foam over when it's opened. We don't want to waste any." I popped the cork and let it fly

Joe jumped up from his chair and caught it with an exaggerated leap, almost knocking over the table. We were both a bit tipsy. "I caught the cork. I get to pour."

"I never heard that rule before."

"That's because I just now made it up," Joe replied and he poured us both a generous glass of the bubbly wine and handed one to me. "It's almost pink! How do you do that?"

"It's blended with four percent syrah grapes from Jillian's sister's winery in New York," I answered. We clicked our glasses and drank.

Joe was silent for a long moment, letting the taste linger on his tongue. "Paradise. This is my idea of paradise. Drinking this, I'm imagining that I'm on a deserted beach on a beautiful Caribbean island with a hot girl, lots of fresh lobster to eat, and a case of Chloe Sparkles to drink. What more could a man want?"

"Ice to keep the wine cold and strawberries," I added. "Or if we're in the Caribbean, maybe mangos instead. Yes, definitely mangos." I was inserting myself in his fantasy as the "hot girl".

"Yeah, mangos work for me, too." He took another sip and leaned back in the chair with his eyes closed and his legs stretched out to the fire. I took the opportunity to study him more closely. I liked what I saw. He seemed completely relaxed and content. Was he imagining me with him on his island paradise?

Joe opened his eyes, catching me staring at him, and smiled slowly, holding my gaze. His eyes were green, no blue, no greenish blue, or maybe bluish green. He looked down at the tray. "Only one bottle left? Nothing can top this one."

I tore my gaze away from his eyes. "Ready for dessert? You can't taste wine on Old Mission without finishing with Cherry Wine." I watched Joe as he tasted it. He smacked his lips appreciatively. I handed him a dark chocolate kiss. "Eat this, then try it again."

Joe looked up from his glass. "Wow", he said. "This reminds me of the cherry pies my grandmother baked when I was a little boy. Wonderful."

"Was your grandmother from near here?" I asked, trying to get a clue about where he was from. "Since this is such a huge cherry producing region, many women around here are well known for their cherry pies."

"No, she lives downstate." Aha, a clue! Only people who live "up north" in Michigan refer to anyplace south of M-55 as "downstate".

Joe glanced at his watch, then out the window. Suddenly, he was all business. "It's getting late. You probably want to close up and I've taken too much of your time. I'll see Tommy another time. I really must go but I would like to buy a couple of bottles of wine. One of Ruby Lips and one of the Chloe wine. I like that one too." He smiled sweetly and I felt a bit of a flip-flop in my chest.

Good, a purchase meant a credit card and a last name. Joe carried the tray back to the counter for me while I got the two bottles for him and rang up the sale. "Can I give Tommy a message for you or would you like to leave a note?" I asked. "I can't imagine what's keeping him."

Joe walked up to the counter and pulled his wallet out of his pocket. "No, thanks. I'll talk to him later, nothing urgent." He handed me a fifty dollar bill. Cash – drat! I gave him his change and bagged the wine for him. "Chloe, thank you for the wine lesson. You kept your promise and made a wine lover out of me." He pulled on his jacket, hat and gloves, picked up the bag and was out the door as I was calling "Please come again," and meaning it. I'd really like to see him again. How was I going to find him if he didn't come back?

His car! The license plate number! I ran to the window overlooking the parking lot. The only car there was mine. No receding tail lights going down the drive. It was still snowing, but not hard enough to instantly cover new tire tracks and there were no tire tracks in the snow. It was as if he had vanished into the gloomy, snowy afternoon.

The phone rang and I pulled myself away from the window to go answer it. "Northern Lights, this is Chloe".

"Chloe, it's Tommy. The roads are getting really bad. Are you busy there?"

"No, not at all," I replied. "Only one customer all afternoon. I think he is a friend of yours, he said he was here to see you. His name is Joe and he didn't leave a message. He just said he would catch you later."

"Thanks, Chloe. Why don't you close up and go home now before the roads get any worse." Tommy was always worried about the girls who worked at the winery, just as if we were his own daughters. Even though Tommy was old enough to be my father, I still thought he was kind of cute. If anyone ever makes a movie of my life, I hope they get Kevin Costner to play Tommy. He'd be perfect for the part.

"Leave Coco in the tasting room. I'll come and get her when I get home. Call me on my cell when you get home. I want to be sure you get there safely. And no detours, go straight home."

"Yes, Dad," I teased him. I was hoping he would say more about Joe, but he was focused on the weather. "See you tomorrow."

"If this keeps up all night, check for school closings tomorrow morning. Don't try to come in until the roads are plowed." That would be nice, give me a chance to sleep in. "I have a meeting tomorrow morning at the Grand Traverse Resort about the reception for the Governors' Conference this summer so I won't be there to open. Just come in and open when you can make it. If you can't get in, neither can the customers."

I said good-bye, hung up the phone, tidied the bar, banked the fire for the night, patted Coco on the head, made sure she had a bowl of fresh water, checked the security system, pulled on my coat and boots and hat and gloves, grabbed my purse, turned out the lights, and locked up behind me. We had at least eight inches of new snow in the parking lot but, thanks to four-wheel drive, a necessity for winter living up here, I was able to get out onto the main road with no problem.

Northern Lights is out on Old Mission Peninsula, a long skinny peninsula that divides Grand Traverse Bay into East and West Bays. It's a perfect climate for grapes and cherries and home to several wineries. Tommy was right, the road was bad, snow-covered and slippery but 20 minutes later, I pulled safely into my parking spot at the condo.

* * *

Bottled Sunshine – Our Chardonnay will tempt you with aromatic hints of apple, pear, and melon. Aging in French oak infuses our Chardonnay with a buttery mouth feel. Liquid gold in a bottle. It's perfect with simple summer suppers and wintertime soups.

Chapter 2

Roses in Winter

Chloe

"Hi, Lil, I'm home," I called out as I shook the snow off my coat and hat and kicked off my boots. I knew Lilianna was home. I could hear the voices of *Friends* coming from the TV in her room. Lilianna is the biggest *Friends* fan I know. She has all 10 seasons on DVD and plays them constantly. She compares every guy either one of us meets to Joey, Ross, or Chandler. "Something smells wonderful! Did you bring dinner home?"

Lilianna is head chef at a great restaurant downtown and often tries out new recipes at home or brings home leftover daily specials. I think she went to cooking school mainly because Monica on *Friends* is a chef and Lil is a brunette like her. Whatever the reason, she is a great cook - and a wonderful friend and roommate.

"Hi, Sparks," Lil came out of her room and joined me in the kitchen. "We were so slow because of the storm that we closed early. You too?" I nodded. "I brought home extra soup of the day for us - Sweet Potato Bisque, and a loaf of zucchini bread to go with it. Are you hungry?"

"I wasn't until I smelled that! Yum!" Lil is my oldest friend. We've been friends our whole lives and she's one of the few people in Traverse City who still calls me Sparks. My birthday is on the Fourth of July and Mom used to put sparklers on my birthday cakes instead of candles.

"That smile on your face isn't just for my soup." Lil was looking at me closely. "What have you been up to? How did you meet a new guy in a snowstorm? What is he, a cop or a tow truck driver? Are you okay? Is your car okay? How did you get home?"

Nothing is secret when you oldest friend is also your roommate, not that I wanted to keep my afternoon with Joe a secret anyway. I was dying to tell someone about him.

"No, nothing like that. He came into the tasting room this afternoon looking for Tommy, who wasn't there, fortunately for me, because I had a terrific private tasting party just for him. Oh, Lil, you know what it's like when you meet someone and you feel so comfortable right away with him that you can just talk and talk for hours and never run out of things to say or have any awkward pauses when you just can't find anything more to say and the silence is just stretching on and on till you know anything you say will sound phony? When you laugh at the same silly things and see in his eyes that he really gets you and is not just being nice to try to get you to bed? Well that's who walked into Northern Lights this afternoon."

"Slow it down a bit, Sparks," Lil said. "Does you new soulmate have a name? Where is he from? What does he do? Where does he live? Did you even find out if he is unattached or did you just check out the ring finger?"

"His name is Joe. No rings. And Coco went crazy over him. He can sing Joni Mitchell songs. His grandmother made cherry pies. And he has dark hair that curls a bit when he sweats and his eyes are kind of blue and kind of green, hazel I guess you call them. And the strangest thing happened when he left. He just disappeared – vanished into the snow."

"Joe with no ring who mysteriously vanishes! He's your kind of guy alright. You talked for hours and that's all you know about him? And just what were you doing to make him sweat?"

I laughed. "What do you think we were doing? Alone by the fire, drinking wine, with the snow storm isolating us from the rest of the world, such a romantic scene. But really, all we did was talk. He was sweating when he came in and pulled off his hat. I guess that is a bit strange. It was freezing out, why would he be sweating? And when he left, I looked out the window for his car, but there was none. No car, no tire tracks left in the parking lot. Nothing! He wouldn't have walked in. There's nothing anywhere nearby to walk from or to. It's very odd. I'm hoping he comes back tomorrow to see Tommy. I'd really like to see him again. If he doesn't come back, how am I going to find him? For once, I wish I'd found out more about a guy on our first date, and this wasn't even a date. Oh my God, this must be serious!"

"It's seriously nuts, Chloe!" Lil was carrying bowls of steaming soup to the table for us. "I've never seen you get so worked up about a guy before. Tomorrow, ask Tommy about him and check him out before you go doing something crazy."

Lil sliced the bread. I poured Bottled Sunshine into two wine glasses and we sat down to eat. The Chardonnay was great with the soup and bread and infused our simple dinner with the taste of a sunny summer day.

I couldn't fall asleep that night. Lil was right, I was acting crazy, but there was something special about Joe that made me want to throw all my dating rules out the window. Here was a guy I wanted to know all about, and all I knew was his first name. I must have finally slept, because I dreamed of a shadowy figure disappearing into a blinding white swirl of snow.

The blinding light was real and coming in through my window. I woke up. It was a *Chelsea Morning* all right. The sun was pouring *in like butterscotch and the first thing on my mind* was Joe. I hadn't just dreamed him. He was real. I just needed to find out who he was.

Morning had brought one of those perfect northern Michigan winter days. The sky was a deep blue and the brilliant sunshine on the new snow was dazzling. I could hear the sounds of the snowplow clearing our parking lot. So much for sleeping in. I switched on the television news to check for any school closings. Everything open and on time. The plows must have been out all night.

I yawned and stretched and looked around my room in appreciation. Dane, Ben's partner, had helped me decorate the condo and we had saved my bedroom for last. Well almost last, Lil's room was her own and done in the simple, neutral colors that she favored. In contrast, my room was a riot of all my favorite hues. We dubbed the style quirky romantic. The walls were pale greenish-blue or bluish-green, depending on the time of day and the light. The drapes were brilliant scarlet, the condo beige carpet was now covered with a beautiful oriental rug in every shade of wine, from deep purple merlot, ruby red cabernet, rosy pink rose, buttery chardonnay, and pale Riesling. The lamp shades were the palest pearly pink, like the soft inside of a conch shell. They gave the room a soft flattering glow. My queen size bed wore a scarlet bed skirt, and a royal purple and cream satiny comforter. The headboard was reproduction French bordello. It made me laugh and feel sexy at the same time.

I got up and pulled off my not-so-sexy flannel pajamas and headed into my bathroom. After my shower, I surveyed my closet and selected my favorite jeans and blue wool sweater to wear. My friend Mandy makes jewelry. For Christmas she gave me a beautiful pair of lapis and silver dangly earrings that perfectly matched the sweater. My friends and I have a pact about gift giving, no spending money when we can make or do it ourselves. Lil gives food, Mandy gives jewelry, Summer gives haircuts, and I give wine. Well I don't exactly make the wine myself, but they all appreciate it and I get a great employee discount. We want to make friends with a good massage therapist.

Thanks to Summer, my hair was cut in a flattering, chin-length bob that fell nicely into place with just a quick blow drying. My makeup takes a bit longer, but worth the effort I had to admit when I did a final check in the mirror.

I followed the aroma of fresh coffee into the kitchen. Not only is Lil a wonderful cook, she makes great coffee too. This morning's brew was a freshly ground hazelnut cinnamon blend.

The kitchen reflected Lil's taste more than mine. The walls were painted a yummy shade of whipped-cream in here and in the open living room and dining area. In the kitchen, Lil kept everything neat and clean, and neutral. Other than the red towels and utensil holder that I had bought, it looked like a restaurant kitchen, just the way she liked it. That was okay with me because she did all the cooking and I reaped the rewards.

But Dane and I had gone wild in the living room. Dane found wallpaper that was a gigantic scale antique map of the world to cover one wall. The colors were muted shades of pink, gold, ivory, blue and green. We hit the jackpot at a local consignment shop with a comfy old sofa, two arm chairs, and a Victorian fainting couch. We had the sofa recovered in plush red velvet and placed it on an old faded oriental rug from the same shop. The two chairs were redone in colorful Suzani prints. I used some of the extra fabric from the chairs to make pillows for the sofa.

For the fainting couch, we found a deep burgundy, almost purple, sensuously silky fabric. The frame was so scratched and dented that instead of trying to bring back the original dark wood finish, we painted it silver and aged it to look slightly tarnished. An ivory cashmere throw was draped casually over the arm.

The dining table and chairs were more consignment store finds. We kept the table's dark finish, but did the chairs in the same silver finish as the couch and recovered the seats in a glowing Mediterranean blue and emerald green print. We kept the window treatments fairly simple with linen panels edged with green ribbon. They gave us some privacy but still let in the light. Added to this mix were various old side tables and crystal lamps that my Grandmother gave me when she moved to Florida.

Over the mantle of the gas fireplace hung an original watercolor of a vineyard on a hill overlooking Lake Michigan. It was by a local artist and I'd fallen in love with it at an art fair last summer. I had another of her paintings in my bedroom. That one was of a mermaid whose iridescent green tail gleamed and long flowing hair didn't quite cover her bare breasts.

You look terrific this morning," Lil said as I poured myself a cup of coffee. "Shame to waste it on digging out your car before you head off to work. The lot has been plowed but our cars are going to be a mess." The condo has no garage and the plow drivers just go around our cars, so we have to dig our way through to them.

I went to the kitchen window overlooking the parking lot. Lil was right. The cars were covered with snow and the plow had left rows of snow around the parked cars. All but one – mine. From our second story window, I could see the roof and hood of my red SUV, all cleared of snow. A neat path was shoveled from the building's door to my driver's side door. And on the hood of my car was something that from up here looked like a pink rose tied with a ribbon.

"Lil", I said. "Come and look at this. What is that on my car? And it's all cleaned off. Who did that?"

Lil joined me at the window and looked down. "Nice, Sparks. Do you have a secret admirer who is into snow removal? Could you ask him to do mine too next time?"

I was pulling on my boots and heading out the door already and didn't answer her. I followed the cleared path to my car and there, waiting for me on the hood, was a perfect pink rose and a silver sparkler tied with a sheer pink ribbon.

"Where does anyone find a sparkler in Traverse City in February?" Lil had followed me outside and her question echoed my own thoughts. The snow clearing and the rose could have been from anyone, but not many people know about my nickname. Who would have left a sparkler with the rose?

"Maybe it's a leftover from the fourth of July. Oh my God! I'll bet it was Joe. He likes the Chloe Sparkles wine."

"What did he do, follow you home last night, go out in a snow storm and buy a rose and a ribbon, and find a leftover sparkler, then come back here early this morning to clear the snow off your car and leave the rose, just because he liked the wine? Didn't you say he didn't have a car? How could he have followed you – on skis? Sounds more like a stalker than a secret admirer." I had to admit that Lil had a point or two, but I just knew somehow that Joe was the one who left the rose.

Before I left, I dug through my music collection for the Joni Mitchell Hits CD. I was going to keep this *Chelsea Morning* going all day.

I never get tired of the drive from home up to Northern Lights. M-37 is the main road running north up Old Mission Peninsula to its tip at Lighthouse Park. The road soars and dips over the hills and through the cherry orchards and vineyards. At spots it follows the shoreline, giving you dramatic views of the ever changing waters of the Bay. It seemed especially beautiful that morning after the snow storm. The sky was a vivid blue and the fresh snow on the ground dazzled in the winter sunshine like it was covered with diamond chips - or sparklers. I was wearing my sunglasses and singing along with Joni's oldies. Mom was forever playing her old Beatles and Stones records when I was growing up and I know all the lyrics to all the oldies. I knew today was going to be a good day. Was it the glorious sunshine or the afterglow of my afternoon with Joe? Was it the sight of that perfect pink rose tied with the silver sparkler that I had put in a vase and brought with me? Whichever, I was feeling fine and flying high. I still didn't know how I was going to find Joe, but I just knew I would see him again, and I had a hunch it would be soon.

The winter sunshine brought the customers. We were exceptionally busy for a weekday in winter. On a day like this, people feel the need to get out of hibernation. Mandy VanDenBrook was working with me and we could barely keep up. Mandy lives just a few miles away with her husband Ted, a computer programmer and web site designer, and their little boy, Connor, a darling little blond cutie. She's been working at the Northern Lights part-time since Connor was born and she also makes jewelry at home, which she sells at the local art fairs in the summer. She's the very talented and creative friend who made my beautiful lapis and silver earrings.

"Do you think we should put out brochures for substance abuse support groups?" Mandy asked me when we had a brief lull mid-morning. "Wine tasting at nine in the morning is just wrong."

"You didn't feel that way before you became a mother, Mandy. I remember some wild nights that lasted well into the next morning when we had Mimosas and Bloody Marys with breakfast. And anyway, it's good for business. Can you believe the sales we've had already today? We need to get these glasses washed and some of these shelves restocked before the next wave comes in." Mandy had noticed the rose and sparkler in its vase on the counter, but had been too busy to ask me about it. I was hoping for a long enough break in the action to tell her all about yesterday and my secret admirer - slash - snow removing stalker if you wanted to go with Lilianna's interpretation of events.

But the next wave of tasters piled in even before we finished washing glasses. A group of cross country skiers headed up to Lighthouse Park stopped in for a few bottles of wine to complete the picnic lunch they had packed. Of course, they wanted to taste everything we sold before they made their selections. Then it was two middle-aged couples who came to Traverse to go to the casinos. The beautiful weather convinced them to spend the day out wine tasting instead of in the casinos. Good choice, I'll take wine over gambling any day. But these four were definitely wine novices. They made puckery faces and complained that the reisling and cabernet was too sour for them and asked if we have any white zin. Mandy very tactfully steered them to the Cherry wine and they left happy with several bottles.

"White zin – yuck. Might as well drink fermented Kool-aid." I carried the tasting glasses to the sink.

The door opened again and a beautiful girl with long red hair and big green eyes walked in. "Hello," she said as I looked up. "Are you Chloe? I'm here for the interview. I'm Skye McAdo." I'd almost forgotten, well okay so I had completely forgotten, but remembered as soon as she said her name. How could anyone forget a name like that? We needed another part-time person and Skye had answered my ad.

"Good morning, Skye. You're right on time. Yes, I'm Chloe and this is Mandy. Let's go into the office so we can talk. Mandy, will you be okay out here by yourself for a little while? Wave at me if it gets crazy. We've had a very busy morning," I said to Skye as I led her to the office. It was just off the tasting room and had a one-way window so whoever was using it could see out into the tasting room.

We discussed her resume and background. She had worked in a winery in southwest Michigan before moving up north last year. She was currently working retail in a big department store and going to school part-time. I'd checked her references before scheduling the interview. "What are you studying?" I asked.

"I'm getting my certification as a massage therapist," she replied. "I've got a few more months of training."

"We'd love to have you join us here at Northern Lights, Skye. When can you start?"

I left Skye in the office filling out paperwork and went to check on Mandy. She was just finishing ringing up a sale for one of our regular, local customers.

"Hello, Mrs. Montgomery," I greeted her. "Stocking up or having a party?" She had two cases of wine on the counter.

"Both, actually," she replied. "Our anniversary is this coming weekend and the kids are all coming up. Forty years together, can you believe it!"

"Oh, I believe it all right. When I find a man as terrific as your husband, I'll be sure to hang on to him. You two are my role models for a perfect marriage."

"Now, Chloe, you are such a romantic. There is no such thing as a perfect marriage. Life is not like a fairy tale. Happily ever after is just an overused phrase to put an ending on a story. Real life starts where the fairy tales end. Happily ever after takes a lot of work. But well worth the effort," she added with a twinkle in her eyes.

Mandy helped carry the boxes out to her car. When she came back in, Skye was just coming out of the office with the completed forms. "Mandy, meet our newest Northern Lights girl, Skye McAdo. She's starting tomorrow and she's going to be a massage therapist soon. Do you know where the camera is?"

We always take a snapshot of our new employees for our newsletter. "Cool," Mandy said as she got the digital camera from under the counter. "We need more help here and a good massage therapist."

I asked Skye to stand by the fireplace for a picture. She looked great in jeans and apricot colored sweater that should have clashed with her red hair but somehow enhanced the color instead. She smiled broadly and I snapped several pictures. "Let's download these and you can choose a favorite."

Mandy followed us into the office. I took the memory card out of the camera and inserted it into the slot in the computer and we all watched and waited for the pictures to come up on the screen.

"Who is that?" Mandy asked as the first picture came up. "It's definitely not Skye."

"Oh, my God! It's Joe!" I exclaimed. "How did this get in here? Who took the pic, when, why, how?" I was baffled.

"Who's Joe," Mandy asked.

"He's cute, is he your boyfriend?" Skye asked.

"Yesterday, he was here. I don't know anything about him except his name – Joe. He came in during the storm, and we talked for hours, and then he vanished. And this morning, my car was cleaned off and that pink rose with the sparkler was left on the hood and I'm sure he was the one who did it. But Lil thinks he's a stalker and I don't know who he is or how he left last night, but I do want to see him again and how come he's in our camera? I didn't take his picture yesterday. Who did? And why?"

"Who's Lil?" Skye asked.

"What do you mean – he vanished?" Mandy asked.

Before I could answer either one of them, the bell over the door tinkled and a new group of customers came in. "Back to work. I'll fill you in later. Skye, if you want to leave now, we can choose your picture tomorrow."

Skye followed us to the tasting counter. "If it's okay with you, I'd like to stay and observe. I'll need to learn your wines and I want to hear more about your mystery guy."

We were so busy for the rest of the morning that Skye offered to go to the Old Mission Deli and pick up sandwiches for all of us for lunch. She came back with turkey ruebens, my favorite, just as the last group of customers was leaving. We pulled up stools behind the bar, opened Diet Cokes and our sandwiches, and between mouthfuls I told them all I knew about Joe, which wasn't much.

Mandy was thoughtful for a moment after I finished my story. "Talk to Tommy, he must know who Joe is. Didn't you say that Joe asked for him when he came in? And if his picture is in the company camera, he must be connected to the Northern Lights somehow. Has Tommy hired anyone new? Jillian would know, she does the newsletter. Where are they today anyway?"

"Jillian is downstate visiting her Mom and Tommy went to a planning meeting with the other wineries for the National Governors' Meeting at the Grand Traverse Resort in July. They are going to do a wine tasting party one evening for all of the governors. It's a big promotion for Michigan wines. I think he'll be gone most of the day."

Skye glanced at her watch. "I've got to run. I have a class at two o'clock. What time do you want me here tomorrow?"

"Can you be here at eight?" I asked. "That will give us time to go over everything before customers start coming in."

"Sure," Skye said. "I'll see you tomorrow. I think I'm going to like working here!" And with that, she was out the door.

Mandy and I were busy the rest of the afternoon. Every time the bell over the door jingled signaling another customer, I hoped it would be Joe coming back to look for Tommy again, or to see me again.

Tommy and Jillian's house is on the Northern Lights property, near the tasting room. If I crane my neck looking out the side window, I can see their driveway and back entrance. There was no sign of their return that afternoon. I tried calling, but there was no answer on their home phone or Tommy's cell phone. Twice, I went back to the office to look at the picture on the computer for clues. I was sure it was Joe, but that was all. The background was a plain white wall. He was wearing a denim shirt with a hint of white tee shirt showing at the neck. That was it. No way to tell who took it, where or why. Just before we left for the day, I pulled up the picture again, printed a copy, and slipped it into my purse. Tomorrow I would find a chance to ask Tommy about him.

The next morning Skye was waiting in the parking lot when I got to work. "You're an early bird. Remind me to give you a key so you can build a fire and have the coffee ready for me next time. Did you have breakfast? My roommate, Lil, is a chef and I brought some of her homemade cinnamon rolls in for us."

"Yum-Oh!" Skye took the box of rolls from me so I could unlock the door and turn on the lights. "I know I'm going to like working here."

"Lil and I have a girl's night at our house every Thursday. Would you like to come tonight? It's just a few friends. Lil makes a big pot of soup or something and we have some wine. It started when we all got together to watch *Friends* on Thursday but we've kept it going since the show ended. Lil has all of the seasons on DVDs and sometimes we pop one in to watch but mostly we just hang out and talk about our love life, or lack of love lives, and laugh a lot. It would be great to have you come too."

"Sounds like fun, I'd love to come." Skye was eyeing the rolls. "I haven't met a lot of people since moving here. How do you stay so slim with a roommate who cooks?"

"Good metabolism and genes, I guess. Everybody tells me it will catch up to me when I turn 30, but for now I seem to be able to eat whatever I want." I craned my neck and looked out the side window to Tommy's house. The garage door was just going down and his Jeep was backing out of the driveway. "Drat! Where is he going now? I really wanted to talk to him this morning." I grabbed the phone and dialed his cell. No answer again. With Jillian not home to remind him, he usually forgot to turn it on and take it with him. I was starting to feel like he was avoiding me.

"Chloe, did you find out anymore about Joe yet?"

"No, and It's driving me crazy. I've always liked men with a little mystery, but this is ridiculous. All I know is his first name. And I just can't figure out how that picture got on our camera here."

"I was thinking about that picture too. May I see it again?" Skye asked.

"Sure, I printed a copy. It's right here," I pulled it out of my purse and handed it to her. She studied it with a small frown. "Do you recognize him?"

Skye hesitated. "Not really, but I could swear I've seen him before somewhere. Maybe a couple of years younger and with his hair a little bit longer and a black turtleneck instead of the denim shirt. Those hazel eyes are so gorgeous. I just can't quite remember. Maybe he just looks like someone I saw in a movie or on TV."

"Ted, Mandy's husband, is a computer programmer. I wonder if he could alter the picture the way you described. Let's send it to him." I set the print of the picture on the counter behind the bar and went into the office.

I booted up the computer and sent Ted the picture with an e-mail asking him if he could make him younger, with longer hair and a different shirt. Skye started the coffee, cleaned yesterday's ashes from the fireplace and soon had a new fire going, making the old stable warm and cozy.

I left my rose and sparkler here on the bar last night when I went home and I reached for the vase to give it fresh water. "Yikes!" I shrieked and Skye came running over.

"What's wrong?" she asked, looking around. "Did you see a mouse or something?"

"My rose," I stammered. "Roses – there was only one yesterday, the pink one. Where did the other one come from?" There were two roses and a sparkler in the vase now – the pink one and a new one in a deeper shade of mauve.

Did Joe come back last night after we closed and leave another rose? How had he gotten in? How did he know I left the rose here yesterday? Maybe Lil was right and he really is a stalker. Or maybe I was just going crazy.

It was close to noon when Tommy finally came into the office wearing a big, goofy looking grin and waving a travel brochure at me. I introduced Skye to him and he welcomed her to the Northern Lights family with a smile. Then he asked us both if we could keep a secret. "I've booked a Caribbean Cruise for Jillian's birthday next month!"

"And you're not going to tell her? She won't be happy about that," I said.

"You don't think she'll like it?" He looked dumbfounded. "She's always wanted to go on a cruise and she's upset about turning 55 so I thought it would be perfect."

"The cruise is perfect. It's keeping it a secret that she won't like. She'll have a lot to do to get ready. She'll need summer clothes and evening dresses and a new bathing suit. She'll need to shop and get a pedicure and a haircut. If you keep it secret, she won't have a chance to get ready. And who is going to pack for you if you don't tell her? You need more than shorts and tees and flip-flops on those cruise ships. Do you have a tuxedo? And Tommy, I'm so glad you are here. I've been wanting to ask you about Joe."

"I used to have a tuxedo, not sure if it will still fit. Why do I need a tux for a cruise? And Jillian needs evening dresses? Are you sure? Maybe you're right, I should tell her. She'll be back tomorrow."

"Cruise passengers get dressed up for the formal dinners on board. You could probably wear a dark suit if you don't want to wear the tux, but believe me, Jillian will definitely want to go full out glam. Now about Joe? Did he get in touch with you yesterday? And why is his picture in our camera? Who is he? And were you here last night with the other rose?"

Tommy shook his head. "What are you talking about? I don't know anyone named Joe. What rose?"

"He came in the afternoon of the big snow storm, looking for you. And when I took Skye's picture the next day, I found a picture of him on our digital camera. Here, I printed a copy." I looked on the counter for the picture.

"Oh, Chloe, I'm sorry," Skye said. "I accidentally spilled some Pinot Noir on it this morning and threw it out. It was soaked and ruined."

"No problem, I can print another one." Tommy followed me into the office. The file with Joe's picture was not on the computer and the memory card was no longer in its slot. "Oh, rats! I must not have downloaded the picture before I sent it to Ted. But the memory card must be here somewhere." But it wasn't back in the camera and I couldn't find it anywhere on the desk.

As I was searching the floor under the desk, the fax machine rang and a fax began printing. It was from Ted. "We asked if Ted could alter the picture some. Skye thought maybe she recognized him from somewhere."

Tommy pulled the paper from the fax machine and laughed. "From where, the funny papers?" He handed me the altered picture that Ted had sent. To make him look younger, he replaced Joe's features with a plump baby face. He had made the hair longer, way longer. It looked like he had cut out a model's long curly hair from a shampoo ad and glued it onto Joe's head. Then he used a marker to draw in a black turtleneck. The only original parts of the picture still visible were the gorgeous hazel eyes gazing at me from the baby's face.

Skye looked over his shoulder. "Hmmmm, that doesn't help much does it?"

"Tommy, you must know who he is. He was asking for you. Who took his picture with our camera? He's about 30 and really cute with hazel eyes and dark hair. About six feet tall."

"Sorry, Chloe," Tommy replied. "I don't know any Joes, except old Joe Hawthorn who has an apple orchard about ten miles from here. I don't think you'd call him cute, unless you like 80 year old guys with 60 inch waists."

The bell tinkled and Skye and I went back to the counter and our newest group of tasters. Trailing behind them, unfortunately, was one of our regulars. Tommy headed to the office with a chuckle, "Here's your boyfriend, Chloe."

I looked up expectantly. Was Joe coming in? "Oh, no," I groaned under my breath.

"Who's that?" Skye whispered to me.

Floyd Dufek is Old Mission Peninsula's village simpleton. Good natured, and overly friendly to everybody, like a big, goofy Labrador Retriever, Floyd made the rounds of the wineries on sunny days for free wine and whatever else he could scrounge. We guessed his age at somewhere between 40 and 60, nobody seemed to know, or care, for sure. He lived with his parents still, on a cherry farm, a few miles up M-37, and worked in the summers picking cherries and in the winters mucking out barns. His clothes looked like he hadn't changed them since the first frost back in October and he radiated an odor of cow shit, sweat, and wine. For some reason, he took a particular liking to me.

"Hi Chloe," Floyd gave me one of his big, goofy grins.

"Good morning, Floyd," I replied. "Why don't you sit down here at this end of the bar where it's more private?" I steered him away from the other customers before his stench drove them back out the door. "I bet you'd like to sample some of our wines today, wouldn't you?"

"I'm very thirsty. I been working hard cleaning up after cows and chickens. That's my job."

"And you do it well, Floyd." I poured him a taste of reisling and slid a small bowl of crackers closer to him. "Are you hungry, too?"

He chugged the reisling and stuffed a handful of crackers into his mouth. "Can I have some more, please?" he asked me, gazing up from his seat with a dopey grin.

This time I gave him apple juice. He didn't seem to notice the difference and it kept him happy without getting him drunk.

We were all busy the rest of the afternoon. Every time the door opened and the bell tinkled I looked up hoping to see Joe walk in again. But he never did and soon it was time to leave. I gave Skye directions to my condo and closed up for the evening, heading home for our Thursday night with the girls.

* * *

Chapter 3

FRIENDS ARE THERAPISTS YOU CAN DRINK WITH

Chloe

Most kids write letters to Santa Claus. I wrote to Prince Charming. I wanted him to give up Cinderella and marry me. I was thrilled, but not at all surprised to get a letter from him in return.

My dear, sweet Chloe,

I was most honored and humbled to receive your letter. I am not deserving of such adoration and affection from you. Alas, sweet Chloe, a romance between us is not possible. I have already given my heart and soul to my beautiful Ella, my Lady of Cinders, who is to be my bride, my wife, and God willing, the mother of my children.

I have faith, sweet Chloe, that when the time is right for you, you will find your own Prince who will love you completely and forever. Until that time, you must prepare yourself by studying hard in school and keeping yourself pure.

I remain your ever-grateful friend,
Prince Charming

I was nine years old when that letter arrived in our mailbox for me and I still have it. Mom made a small pink satin pouch tied with ribbon and closed with a rhinestone button to hold it safely. I'm pretty sure that my Dad wrote it and put it in the mailbox for me to find. That stuff about studying hard and keeping myself pure sure sounds like him. But it's sweet that he went to so much trouble for me. The letter is beautifully written on heavy cream colored paper bordered with royal purple. The stamp was foreign looking with the profile of a handsome man wearing a crown. I was sure it was Prince Charming himself.

I've been on the lookout for my Prince Charming ever since then. I've kissed a whole lot of frogs and some guys that maybe were Dukes or Lords, but no Prince...yet.

Why was I thinking of that old letter and Prince Charming tonight? The letter was still safely stored in its pink satin pouch in the bottom of my hope chest. Yes, I know it's corny and old-fashioned but I have a hope chest. It's really more of a cedar chest for holding my wool sweaters and blankets, but I've had it since I was very little and have always thought of it as my hope chest. I guess I'm sort of corny and old-fashioned too.

Lil and I did a quick clean up of the condo before the girls all got there. For our dinner, she had a big pot of boeuf bourguignon bubbling in the oven and another pot of fluffy white potatoes on the stove. I opened a bottle of Aurora Pinot Noir and put a bottle of Bottled Sunshine Chardonnay on ice and set the table, humming *Chelsea Morning* as I did.

Mandy arrived first with a tray of veggies and dip followed quickly by Summer carrying a chocolate torte to die for. They dropped their coats and boots and headed to the kitchen. The doorbell rang again, announcing Skye.

"Hi, Chloe," She smiled at me and handed me a bottle of wine. "I brought a cabernet from the winery in Kalamazoo where I used to work."

"Great! Thank you! We always like to try out our competitors' wines. Come on in and meet Summer and Lil."

Mandy and Summer were on stools in the kitchen munching on carrot sticks and watching Lilianna put the finishing touches on dinner. "Lil, Summer, this is Skye. She's our new Northern Lights girl and is going to be a massage therapist soon. Lil is a fantastic cook and Summer is the best stylist in Traverse City. She has her own little shop downtown called Summer Time. Hey, you girls should be partners in a spa when Skye graduates. You could call it Summer Skyes." That got a laugh from everyone.

"Welcome to our Thursday night girl friends club, Skye," Summer said. "You sure don't need my services. That is the most gorgeous red hair I have ever seen."

Lil smiled, "Don't mind Chloe. She is always coming up with crazy names. She wants Tommy to plant syrah grapes so he can make a wine named after his sister, Kay."

Skye looked puzzled for a moment then laughed. "Don't tell me – Kay Syrah Syrah, right? I like it! People remember fun, catchy names. It's a good marketing tool for wine."

"I knew I liked you right away. It'll be nice to work with someone who thinks like me. Let's open that bottle you brought and get this party started. Who wants what? We have pinot, cab, or chardonnay." We all poured ourselves a glass of wine and helped Lil carry the serving dishes to the table. I clicked on the television and DVD player and *Friends* quietly played in the background while we ate, drank, talked, and laughed. On Thursday nights, I did not miss having a man in my life one bit. But the talk, as usual, soon turned to men.

"What did you find out about your new mystery guy, Chloe? Did he come back today to see Tommy?" Mandy asked as she poured another glass of the Kalamazoo Cabernet. "I like this wine, Skye. Not as much as ours, of course, but a very big flavor – hints of blackberry and licorice – nice." I filled Lil and Mandy in about the strange appearance of the second rose. "Tommy said he doesn't know him and no, he hasn't been back. I don't have a clue who he is or how to find him if he doesn't come back. I don't even have enough information to Google him."

"How about wanted posters plastered up around town?" Lil suggested. "I can see it now – 'Crazy girl seeks mystery man. Hazel eyed, dark haired wine drinker went missing in the storm. Please return to Northern Lights for wine and romance'. We'll do a border of sparklers and pink roses so he'll know you know".

"Great idea! Will you put them up in the restaurant and the businesses downtown? And Summer, you can pass them out in the salon. I'll cover all the wineries on Old Mission and Skye can take them to her school and Mandy, will you see if Ted can post it on-line. Maybe I should do a web-site." I could see Lil and the others laughing at me.

"You can't be serious! You'll have every weirdo in the county flocking up to Northern Lights. I was joking. Good thing you have me to put the brakes on every time you come up with a crazy scheme."

"It was your crazy scheme, Lil. I'm getting desperate. What if he's the one and I never find him again? You've got Evan. You've had Evan forever and he's crazy in love with you, and you've known forever that you two would get married eventually and be together forever." Lil and Evan McQuick started dating in High School and were still together, even though she lived with me in Traverse City and he lived in East Lansing, going to school at Michigan State University. He's going to be a Vet when he finishes school in the spring. They are getting married in June and I will lose my roommate. Maybe that was why I was feeling so desperate to find my own Mr. Right soon. It wasn't just Valentine's Day looming nearer on the calendar. I needed a date for the wedding, and maybe a new roommate.

Lil and I cleared away the main course dishes while Summer served the torte. Skye took a bite and moaned softly. "This is the best meal I've had since I moved here. Thank you so much for inviting me. What do you call this cake?"

Summer replied quickly, "Better than Brad Pitt."

Lil added, "Better than Joey, Ross and Chandler put together. But not better than Evan." She looked at me. "Who's going to play your Joe in your movie?"

"Hmm…none of the above. As sexy as Matthew McConaughey, as McDreamy as Patrick Dempsey, as cute as Josh Hartnett, no - cuter than him. I know - Jake Gyllenhaal! He's gorgeous. Or maybe Jude Law without the English accent."

"What movie are you talking about?" Skye asked.

"Oh, we have this long running game of who is going to be in the movie of our lives. Reese Witherspoon is starring in mine, as me, of course. I've been waiting for my leading man," I explained. "Courtney Cox will play Lil, but she'll have to cut her hair in this short spiky shag like Lil's and Matthew Perry will play Evan, her fiancée. Summer will be Angelina Jolie and Mandy will be Jennifer Aniston."

"Quite a cast," Skye replied. "Who will you get to play me?"

"Nicole Kidman, of course! Another beautiful red-head."

From that point the talk turned to movies, which ones we loved, which ones we hated, and our all-time favorites. *Pretty Woman*, we all decided, was the all-time best chick flick. What girl didn't love the shopping scene?

"My favorite part is when Julia Roberts is having her carpet picnic of champagne and strawberries and watching Lucy stomp grapes on the television while Richard Gere sits back and watches her laugh," I said. "I always wanted to try grape stomping, but Tommy says it's a waste of good grapes."

Skye was quiet for a moment then jumped up and shouted, "That's it. That's who Joe's picture reminds me of!"

"Richard Gere?" I asked, puzzled.

"No, no. The grape stomping reminded me. One of my girl friends in Kalamazoo had this crazy romance novel that was set in a winery and had very sexy parts with the wine maker and various girls in vats of grapes. They did a whole lot more than stomp. It was the sexiest thing I ever read and part of the reason I applied for a job in a winery. The crazy thing was that the author was a young guy who supposedly wrote it on a bet. His picture was on the back cover and that's the picture I was thinking of when I said Joe looked familiar. But I can't remember his name, or the name of the book."

"Call your friend in Kalamazoo. If you can get his name or the name of the book, we can Google him."

Skye pulled her cell phone from the pocket of her jeans, looked up her friend on her contacts and hit call. She waited. We all waited. "Rats, voice mail. She's not answering." When the voice mail message ended, she spoke again. "Katy, it's me, Skye. I need your help with something. I know you'll remember the sexy wine book that we all passed around and read. I really need to know the name of it or the name of the author or both. Even better, can you fax a copy of the author's picture to me at my new job?" She looked at me and I gave her the number. She repeated it into the phone. "Call me please. I miss you, but I'm having a great time up here. Come and see me soon. I've got some new friends who would like you, and your book."

Now we wait. I suppose it's a long shot that Skye's author is actually Joe, but it's the only lead I have.

* * *

Chapter 4

911

Chloe

Friday morning I was up early and very eager to get to work and check for a fax. Lil was still sleeping so I bagged up some of her homemade dried cherry scones for breakfast and drove up to Northern Lights as the sun was coming up. I let myself into the tasting room and went straight to the office to check the fax. Nothing. I started the coffee. Skye wasn't due in until almost ten. I was hoping she had received a call back from Katy. The roses were still in the vase on the bar. Two roses, pink and mauve, and a sparkler. I'm not sure if I was relieved or sorry that a third rose had not mysteriously appeared.

I started the fire in the fireplace, poured myself a mug of coffee, munched on a scone, and tackled some paperwork in the office. The camera was still sitting on the desk. That reminded me. Jillian was due back today. Hopefully, she would know about Joe's picture in the Northern Lights' camera.

Thirty minutes later, the bell jingled. I looked up to see Tommy walking in. He was dressed for the outdoors in a snowmobile suit and Pac boots. "Morning, Chloe," he greeted me. "Coffee smells good. I think I'll take a go cup. Ummm. Can I have one of these scones, too?"

I nodded, "Sure, Lil made them."

"I'm taking the snowmobile up to the ridge. Some pinot vines up there need pruning and tying. If I'm not back by noon, send out a search party." He poured his coffee, added some cream from the wine cooler, snapped on the lid and was out the door. I heard the sound of the snowmobile starting up then fading away as he headed up into the hills. Then it was quiet again and I went back to my paperwork.

At first I didn't pay attention to the sounds coming from Tommy and Jillian's house. On quiet mornings like this, I was used to hearing the sound of their garage door opening and Tommy's Jeep backing out and coming down the drive. It took a couple of minutes to register that Jillian was still gone and Tommy had just left on the snowmobile. Who was driving the Jeep? I ran to the window just in time to see Tommy's Jeep pull out of the drive and turn south, toward town. Grabbing the phone as I ran to the door, I caught a glimpse of the driver. It was a man - that much I could tell, and he was wearing a dark knit cap. I hit the speed dial for Tommy's cell phone, but of course there was no answer. He'd forgotten it again. Drat.

I dialed 911. "This is Chloe Applewhite at Northern Lights. Someone just stole Tommy North's Jeep right out of his garage. He's heading south on 37."

* * *

Ruby Lips – A mature and full bodied blend of the best of the red wines. Lusciously loaded with intense flavors of ripe berries, firm pears, and rich satiny chocolate. A wine to warm you like a lover's kiss on a cold winter night.

Chapter 5

FLASHING

Jillian

Hello. My name is Jillian North. My husband, Tommy, and I own and operate the Northern Lights Winery near Traverse City, Michigan. Chloe Applewhite is the manager of the tasting room and retail store at Northern Lights.

Chloe recently wrote about the events of this past year and asked me to add a few pages to her story - telling the story from my point of view. I haven't done any writing since college comp courses, except for the Northern Lights Newsletters, but Chloe convinced me I could do it and made it sound like fun. So here I go…

I was holding the steering wheel with my knee while unzipping my jacket with one hand and rolling down the car window with the other. Why was I wearing this heavy jacket in the car anyway? And a wool sweater, a turtleneck, jeans, warm socks and boots? I should have at least thrown the jacket in the backseat before I left Mom's house. How could I have forgotten such a simple thing?

I felt the too familiar flush creep up my neck and face and the sweat forming under my breasts and pooling in my lower back.

Taking slow, deep breaths, I looked for a place to pull off the road to cool down. The blast of cold February air coming in from the open window just wasn't doing it. I had to get the damn jacket off. I pulled into a parking lot and threw the car into park as I ripped wildly at the offending jacket and only managed to tangle it in the seat belt that, in my haste to undress, I had forgotten to unbuckle.

"Damn, damn, damn," I muttered in frustration. Finally, I clicked open the seat belt and managed to get the jacket off. The sweater followed. I opened the door and stepped out of the car.

"Oh no", I moaned as I saw where I was. The memory lapses were bad, the constant hot flashes were horrible, but the cravings for sweets were driving me absolutely crazy. My jeans were already too tight, but here I was in the parking lot of Judy's Pies - the best pies south of Traverse City – and my overheated, sweat-drenched body wanted apple pie. It wanted a whole pie, a Dutch apple pie with a crumb topping, and a fork to eat it with.

I was just grabbing my purse to start walking across the parking lot when my cell phone rang. Saved by the bell. I sat back down in the car, fumbled in my purse and looked at the caller ID – my sister.

"Hi Jackie", I answered the phone. "Please distract me from my pie cravings. I'm about to give in."

"Are you still at Mom's?" Jackie asked. "I thought you'd be on your way home by now. Did she bake a pie for you?"

"No, I left half an hour ago and made it to Linwood. I'm having a flash in the parking lot of Judy's Pies. I had to pull over to get my coat off and here I am. Too convenient."

Jackie chuckled. She understood all too well, being a few years older than me and having undergone the hot flashes of menopause herself. Jackie lives in upstate New York and runs Wild River Winery with her husband and sons. They are the ones who convinced Tommy and me to go into the wine business for ourselves.

"Jillian, get back in your car and forget the pie. How's Mom? Did you talk to her about our plan?"

"Mom's great, she's doing better than me. She's too busy with her social life to be an old lady. Dance classes, yoga classes, computer classes, volunteering at the elementary school, driving her friends all around town to their appointments. She's even organizing trips for seniors, including a wine tour up in Grand Traverse. If she does come to your place, it will be with a busload of octogenarians ready to drink wine and dance all night. She just laughed when I suggested that she consider coming to live with us or with you. You know what she told me? '80 is the new 50!' That makes her younger than us. I'm exhausted from trying to keep up with her for the past few days. I'm going home to work and relax."

I heard Jackie's sigh over my cell phone. "Are you sure that it's not all too much for her? I appreciate you going to check on her so often. I worry because I'm so far away. She's 80 years old. She should have her family around her to take care of her."

"Are you sure you don't want her at Wild River to take care of you and Dan and the boys? She is a better cook than either of us."

"Dan and I both gained ten pounds last time she visited. David is away at school, and Devlin is up at your place. I hope he and Tommy haven't devoured everything in the place while you were gone."

"What's Dev doing at our place? When did he come? This is the first I've heard of it." I was puzzled. I loved my nephew, Devlin, but hadn't seen him since our last visit to New York and had no clue that he was coming to Michigan. "Mom didn't mention it either."

"Oh, no big deal," Jackie replied. "Dev just wanted to take some time off during our slow season. He went skiing at Boyne Mountain with some friends from school and dropped in on Tommy a couple of days ago. Tommy must have been lonely without you and asked him to stay."

"Tommy must have forgotten to mention it. I hope he's still there when I get home. It's been too long since I've seen him. I think my pie craving has passed and I'm cooled off now. I'm going to get driving again. Don't worry about Mom, she's fine."

We chatted for a couple more minutes about the weather and who had the most snow then hung up. Soon I was back on the road headed north toward Pinconning and Standish. My car is a classic Jaguar and I try to avoid driving it on the expressway whenever possible. So I take the long way on the state roads. My cell phone rang again. This time it was a number that I didn't recognize. But I knew the voice on the other end of the line.

"Aunt Jilly?" he said. "I'm being arrested."

"What? Devlin, what happened? Where is Tommy?"

"Uncle Tommy took the snowmobile and went up in the vineyard to prune. He asked me to take the Jeep and run into town for a few things and Chloe must have seen me leave and reported it stolen. She doesn't know I'm here. The cops stopped me a few minutes ago. Tommy's not answering his cell phone, so I called you. Can you please straighten this out?"

"Put the officer on the phone and I'll talk to him. Tommy should have introduced you to Chloe and told her you were using the Jeep."

Luckily, the officer who stopped Devlin was a customer who knows me and took my word that he was my nephew and had permission to drive the Jeep. I'll have to try to remember to offer him a complementary bottle next time he comes in, or is that bribery? Poor Devlin, he sounded very upset. He's such a good kid, he's probably never even had a parking ticket, let alone almost being arrested for auto theft. It is odd that Chloe didn't know about him being there.

* * *

Sugar & Spice – And all things nice is this Michigan gewurtztraminer. Lively and refreshing. Lots of fresh fruit flavors, a hint of spice, and a lingering finish.

Chapter 6

DIBS ON DEVLIN

Chloe

What a crazy day!

First, Tommy came back from the vineyards and when I told him about the Jeep being stolen, he burst out laughing. Then he proceeded to tell me about his nephew staying with him while Jillian was gone and how he sent him out with the Jeep. He could have saved us all a lot of trouble if he'd told me that earlier.

Second, Jillian came back and laid into Tommy for not telling me about the nephew, whose name is Devlin by the way, and for forgetting his cell phone whenever she wasn't around to remind him. I hope they didn't leave a mess in the house. That will really send her over the edge. She was so hot, I didn't even want to ask her about the picture of Joe in the camera, and I've been dying to do that. Hopefully, the two cherry scones she grabbed on her way out the door will cool her off. Lately, she's been acting kind of crazy.

Third, Skye came in all excited because her friend Katy had called her about the book she was looking for. She couldn't find the book or remember the author's name but the book was called *Sweet Intoxications*. As soon as we get a break in the customers here, we're going to Google it and see what we can find.

Fourth, the phone rang and it was my little sister, Clementine, telling me she was at the airport in Traverse City and needed somebody to pick her up.

"Clemmie, what are you doing at the airport? Why aren't you in school?" I asked.

"It's winter break here and all my friends went to Cancun. Mom and Dad wouldn't let me go, so I got a ride to the airport and came up here to see you. I don't want to spend winter break hanging around at home. Even staying with you is better than that."

"You flew from Bay City to Traverse City?"

"It's okay. I had enough money for the ticket and it was kind of fun. There was no direct flight today, so I got to go to Chicago first and then here. I love flying into Chicago over Lake Michigan. It's so beautiful. I almost stayed there, but I didn't have anybody there to stay with. Can you come and pick me up?"

That's the way Clemmie operates. Head in the clouds and no plans beyond the present. "I can't leave right now. We're very busy here. Let me see if Lil can get away to come get you. I'll call you back."

I hung up the phone and shook my head. Tommy looked at me. "Is Clementine here?"

Tommy and Jillian had met Clemmie last summer when she came up to spend a weekend with me.

"Yeah, she's at the airport and needs a ride. This is her idea of running away from home when she doesn't get her way. Mom and Dad wouldn't let her go to Cancun with her friends."

"Devlin can go get her for you," Tommy offered. "As long as you don't sic the cops on him again."

"That would be great. Are you sure he won't mind after I tried to have him arrested?"

"No problem. Rescuing damsels in distress is his specialty."

"Clemmie is more like a nutty teen queen in confusion, but she sure needs rescuing. Thanks, Tommy. I really want to apologize to Devlin in person. I'll call Clemmie and let her know."

I redialed Clemmie's phone. "Tommy's nephew will be coming for you. His name is Devlin. Watch for a green Jeep Grand Cherokee. The license plate is NLWINE. Got that? Do not get in without checking the plate. What are you wearing so he'll recognize you?"

"You're getting as bad as Mom," Clemmie replied. "I know not to get into cars with strangers. I'm wearing my blue North Face jacket,

Gap jeans, Ugg boots and, a hot pink knit cap and gloves from Anthropology. See you soon. Bye." And she clicked her phone off. Clemmie doesn't wear anything without the right label. She didn't mention it, but I'm sure her undies are Victoria's Secret.

I repeated Clemmie's wardrobe descriptions to Tommy. "What in the world are Ugg boots?" he muttered and he went to dispatch Devlin as another group of customers came into the tasting room.

Would I ever get a chance to get to the computer and Google *Sweet Intoxications*?

Skye and I had a steady stream of customers all afternoon. When I finally had a break, I went into the office only to find that Jillian was busy on the computer and the phone – the window wide open and cold air pouring in. No chance to Google or to talk to her.

It was close to five o'clock and I was pouring Sugar & Spice for one of our regular customers, when the door opened and Clementine bounced in dragging her overstuffed backpack. Even if she is my baby sister, I have to tell you Clemmie is a knockout. Today, she looked like Pippi Longstocking with long blond braids swinging freely from under her bright pink knit cap. She's almost six feet tall and slender as the fashion models in my Vogue magazine, even without airbrushing. Her brilliant blue eyes matched her jacket and her cheeks were flushed a pretty pink from the cold. The shaggy bulk of the Ugg boots emphasized the slenderness of her long, denim-clad legs

"Why didn't you tell me Devlin was such a doll? I may never go home again!" she gushed, then ran over to the fireplace to greet the dog. "Coco, how's the sweetest doggie in Michigan?" Coco rolled over to have her belly scratched. Clemmie looked back over at me. "Oh, that looks good. Can I have some?"

"Hi, Clemmie. Nice to see you too," I replied. "And no, the drinking age in Michigan is 21, remember? How about some apple juice instead?"

"Okay, if that's my only choice but can't you give me just a little wine? I want to celebrate. I think I'm in love. He is the cutest guy ever, and don't tell me he's too old for me. I'm almost eighteen, you know."

I rolled my eyes. "How could I not know? You never miss a chance to remind everybody of your birthday. Three more years before I can give you wine." I poured some apple juice into a wine glass for her. " Actually, I haven't met Devlin yet. I just found out he was here before he went to get you. I hope you remembered to thank him."

Clemmie giggled, "Oh, I thanked him alright. Why do you think it took us so long to get here? He may never recover."

"Clemmie! What did you do now?" I gasped.

"Just kidding. I was a very polite and proper little girl. But remember, I saw him first, so I have dibs."

"You can't do dibs on a guy, it doesn't work that way. And besides, he's too old for you and he lives in New York and will be going home soon. You just blew your money on a ticket to Traverse, I don't think you'll be flying to New York next. Let me just clean up and check with Jillian then we can get out of here. It's been a long day and I want to make a stop on the way home. You better call Mom and let her know you got here all right." Clemmie looked chagrinned. "You did tell her you were coming, didn't you?"

"Not exactly. But I'll call her now." She pulled her cell phone from her jeans pocket and hit a speed dial number for home. "It's busy. I'll try back later. Mom never uses her call waiting." She pressed another button. "I have to tell Brittany about Devlin. What time do you think it is in Cancun?"

Before I could figure it out and answer, she was yakking away to her BFF and ignoring me.

Skye assured me she could do the clean up and shooed us out the door. Jillian was still bent over the keyboard, phone in her ear, so I just waved to her and left. Clemmie followed, craning her neck for a glimpse of Devlin at the house. "I just need to stop at the bookstore," I told Clemmie.

By the time we brushed the new snow off my car, warmed it up and cleared the windows, it was full dark outside. By the time we got to Front Street and the bookstore, it was closed. "Drat! Let's go home and try Google."

"What are you looking for?" Clemmie asked and I gave her a quick recap of my afternoon wine tasting with Joe, the roses, the picture, and Skye's idea about the book.

"You're such a dork!" was her reply to my story. "Why didn't you just ask him for his name and number? Girls can do that now, you know. It's not like the Fifties or in the old movies where the girls always sat at home and waited for a boy to call. Guys even like it now when you call them."

Great, just what I need, dating advice from my baby sister. Or maybe that is what I need. I don't seem to be doing so well with my methods.

Lil was leaving as we came in. "It's Evan's break, too," she said, "and I'm going down to Lansing to see him for a few days. Clemmie, you can have my room."

As Clemmie dropped her bag in the living room, her phone rang. "Hi, Mom. I'm at Chloe's if you're wondering." She paused and I could hear our mother's voice coming through the speaker of Clemmie's phone. "No, I got a ride to the airport and flew up. It's okay, I had enough money for my ticket." Pause. "No, one way." Pause. "No, do you want to come and get me or maybe Chloe can take me home. I don't have to be back in school till next Monday." Pause. "Chloe, Mom wants to talk to you."

I took the phone. "Hi, Mom. And before you ask, I didn't know she was coming." Pause. "It's okay with me. We'll have fun catching up. Do you want to come up next weekend and get her?" Pause. "Great, we'll see you Friday and don't worry, I'll try to keep her out of trouble." I clicked off. "Sister, you are in big trouble. She is mad. And I don't think you're too old to be grounded. What were you thinking just flying off without telling anybody? What if I weren't here to get you? Where would you have gone then?"

Clemmie shrugged, "You're always here. Where else would you be? Can't I always count on my big sister?" She batted her blue eyes and I laughed. She always knew how to get her way. Well, almost always. She was in Traverse City instead of Cancun.

We hung up our coats and Clemmie followed me to the desk where I logged onto the internet and Googled *Sweet Intoxications*.

51

"This is no help. A rose and song lyrics from *The Phantom of the Opera*. No steamy romance book about wine making. Or maybe the rose was a clue. If it were, it made no sense to me."

"If it's a book you're looking for, try Amazon," Clemmie suggested. I did and there it was – *Sweet Intoxications* by Devlin Carmichael, new paperbacks priced at $14.99, no used copies available. A picture of the book cover, no picture of the author.

"Devlin!" Clemmie and I both said the name together. "My Devlin?" Clemmie added.

"He's not your Devlin, and it can't be the same guy, can it? That would be too weird a coincidence and anyway, the guy I'm looking for is named Joe."

"I've got dibs, remember, I saw him first."

"If Devlin and Joe are the same person, I saw him first." I thought for a moment then asked, "What exactly does Devlin look like?"

Clemmie sighed. "He's just a bit taller than me, which is perfect for me. He has dark hair, which is perfect for me. Oh, and he has these beautiful eyes. But I'm not sure if they are blue or green. He kept looking at the road while he was driving instead of looking at me."

I ordered the book and paid extra for express shipping.

* * *

Chapter 7

WARMING THE SHEETS

Jillian

Like many old houses in Michigan, the upstairs of our old farmhouse was not adequately insulated. It can be miserably hot in the summer and miserably cold in the winter. Right now, the cold suited me just fine. I slipped between the sheets next to Tommy and snuggled up close to share my body heat with him.

"Mmmmm, you feel good," he moaned. "I missed you. It's was too cold sleeping without you."

"Is that all you missed, my heat?"

Tommy rolled over and gathered me into his arms. I could feel the heat radiating from my body to his and I ran my hands over his chest.

"I missed the softness and heat of your mouth, your Ruby Lips," he said, kissing me deeply. "I missed the softness and heat of your breasts," he said, cupping them firmly in his hands. "I missed the softness and heat of your butt," he said grasping my backside and pressing me to him. I really must do something about the softness of my backside. Several days of Mom's cooking hadn't helped any, but right at the moment, I had other things on my mind. I'd missed Tommy too and while he appreciated my softness, I appreciated his hardness.

"I have a surprise for you," Tommy said later, as the sweat was cooling from my body and he was pulling the comforter back onto the bed from the floor where it had fallen. After all these years of marriage, Tommy still looked great to me. His body was very fit for a man in his mid-fifties. Winemaking may sound like a glamorous career, but there is a lot a hard physical work involved and that work keeps Tommy's muscles toned and his belly flat. His eyes were as deep blue as Lake Michigan on a summer day. His nose was ever so slightly crooked and he had deep dimples on either side of his generous mouth when he smiled or laughed, which he did a lot. His sandy colored hair was receding a bit at the top, but the little bits of grey that were starting to show only added a silvery sheen that was very flattering.

"I was planning on waiting till your birthday to tell you, but Chloe, Mandy and Skye convinced me you would rather know now. I know you've been dreading turning 55, so I booked a special vacation for the two of us to celebrate."

"Oh, Tommy! That's so sweet. Thank you! Where are we going?" Alaska, Antarctica, the North Pole, a menopausal woman could hope.

Tommy nuzzled my neck, "How does a cruise to the Caribbean sound? Just you and me, and about a thousand other people on a luxury cruise ship to St. Thomas, Aruba, and a bunch of other tropical islands. One week of no snow and no work, gourmet dinners and sampling someone else's wine."

Seven whole days of sweltering heat and stuffing my plumped-up figure into a bathing suit, is what I thought of it, but Tommy looked so happy with his surprise that I couldn't spoil it for him. "That sounds incredible! What about Northern Lights? Can we leave for that long?"

"I've got that covered," Tommy replied, excited as a kid at Christmas. "Devlin is going to come back and oversee things for us while we are gone. Jackie and Dan can spare him from Wild River."

I laughed. "He agreed to come back after Chloe almost had him arrested? And why didn't you tell Chloe he was here and introduce them? I'll bet they would really hit it off. Wouldn't they make a great couple?"

"I was going to introduce them. Dev was with me in the office, watching Chloe through the window. He asked me about her and I told him about her crazy mystery man dating theory. You know, how she doesn't want to know anything about a guy before she goes out with him. Then Dev got a phone call and went off with one of his buddies for a bit and I forgot all about telling Chloe he was here. Too bad he has to leave in the morning, but he'll be back next month when we go on our vacation. They'll get a chance to meet each other then."

* * *

Chapter 8

CLUES

Chloe

"Clemmie, wake up. I have to go to work this morning. What do you want to do? If you come with me, I could use your help. We have a special tasting event on the Peninsula today and it should be busy." I shook Clemmie, trying to wake her up. She is not a morning person.

"You work on Saturday?" she asked. "Weekends are for sleeping in."

I tried another tack. "Devlin might be there."

"I'm up. I'm up. Give me a minute to shower and I'll be ready." She jumped out of bed and dashed into the bathroom. I really hope Devlin and Joe are not the same guy. It's weird to think about competing for a man with my baby sister. And, like I said earlier, Clemmie is a knockout.

Ten minutes later, Clemmie, dressed in jeans and a black turtleneck sweater, bounced into the kitchen. "Do you have any of Lil's goodies for breakfast?" she asked. "I'm famished."

"I've got muffins all ready in a bag and two hot cocoas in go mugs," I replied. "Let's get going. I need to be there early to set up. We have wine and food pairings from local restaurants at all the wineries on the Peninsula today. You can't pour or sell wine because you're not eighteen yet, but you can help out with the food and keep us in clean glasses. I'd really appreciate it and you might even have fun doing it."

"Washing wine glasses is not my idea of fun. Neither is getting up so early on a Saturday, but if Devlin is there it will be worth it," Clemmie said, reaching into the bag for a cherry muffin. "Do you think it's too early in Cancun to call Britney?"

Jillian was already starting to set up the tables when we arrived at Northern Lights. Stella, the manager of Old Mission Deli, was helping her. They were doing the food for us today. Customers buy a special pass for tasting food and wine at all of the Old Mission Peninsula wineries for the day. Each winery has a different restaurant partner. It was a beautiful day and we were hoping for a good turnout for the event.

Clemmie was checking around the tasting room and I could guess who she was looking for. "Good morning, Jillian. We never got a chance to talk yesterday. How was your trip downstate?" I asked. I had some other questions for her too, but they could wait. "Clemmie came along to help today."

"That's great! Thanks, Clementine. The trip was good, my mom is doing fine and she fed me too much, as usual. I was surprised when my nephew called me and told me he was being arrested for stealing Tommy's car." Jillian looked at me. "Thanks for keeping an eye on things here, Chloe. I've already talked to Tommy about not letting you know Devlin was here and for not keeping his cell phone with him."

Clemmie was still looking around. "Is Devlin going to be helping today, too?" she asked.

Jillian saw the excitement in her eyes and shook her head slowly. "I'm sorry, Clementine. He had to go back to New York. Tommy took him to the airport this morning. You just missed them." Clemmie's excitement turned to dismay at Jillian's words.

"But he'll be back next month," she continued. "Tommy and I are going on a cruise and Devlin is going to come and oversee things for us here while we are gone."

Clemmie perked up at that. "A cruise – to the Caribbean? How great is that!"

Jillian sighed. "Not my first choice for a vacation right now, but Tommy is really excited about it. He said he wanted to surprise me but you girls talked him out of that. Thank you, Chloe. I need some time to get ready. I don't have any warm weather clothes that fit, let alone a decent bathing suit, and dresses for formal dinners. I really need to do some shopping."

"Lucky you!" Clemmie was really excited now. "Can I help? I love to shop and I'm really good at it. I want to study fashion and journalism and maybe marketing next year in college so I can work for a fashion magazine."

This was the first time I'd heard that Clementine had any plans beyond the end of the week.

Clemmie was looking closely at Jillian. "You've got a classic hourglass figure. Very hot. And with your dark hair and eyes, you should be wearing very strong deep colors. Think jewel tones - emerald green, ruby red, dark sapphire, topaz. We need to accentuate your breasts with wrap styles and low v-necklines. You're lucky that Traverse City has great little shops downtown and consignment shops too. We can find wonderful things for you right here in town. Can we start tomorrow?"

Jillian looked amused. "I'm always hot but do you think you can make me look sexy?"

"You are sexy, voluptuous even. You just need the right clothes to make you feel sexy."

Clemmie was right. Jillian thought she was overweight, but really she looked great. I've got Sela Ward in mind to play her in my movie.

"Tomorrow is Sunday, the shops are closed. How about Monday?"

"It's a date! I'm here all week with nothing to do but shop for you, and maybe I'll shop a little bit for myself too. This is going to be fun!"

"Since you're going to be helping us today, Clementine, why don't you choose a fleece or sweatshirt with the Northern Lights logo for yourself. They're over on the display by the window," Jillian said. "We've got some very nice ones. Pick whatever you would like. My treat."

"Cool, thanks!" Clemmie bounced off, happy with her shopping plans. She selected a purple fleece vest with the Northern Lights logo and slipped it on over her black turtleneck.

"Well, she got over being heartbroken about not seeing Devlin again today in a hurry," I told Jillian.

"Chloe, I'm sorry you didn't get a chance to meet him this trip since you'll be working closely together next month, but I'm sure you'll like him. He's a great kid, even if he is my nephew, and very experienced in the wine business."

I had to ask, "Jillian, what's Devlin's last name?"

She looked surprised. "Didn't I ever tell you about my sister and her family running Wild River Winery in New York? Devlin has been working with them since he was a teenager. He got his degree in viticulture at NYU. Their last name is Carmichael."

Devlin Carmichael, the author of *Sweet Intoxications,* was Jillian's nephew! Was he also the guy named Joe who spent a snowy afternoon tasting wine by the fireplace with me? He must be. Skye recognized him from the picture. If so, why did he use a false name, and why act like he didn't know about wine, and why not tell me who he was? True, I find a bit of mystery attractive when I meet a guy, and I found Joe to be very attractive, but this was ridiculous. And to top it off, I called the police and told them he stole Tommy's Jeep. I almost got him arrested.

Maybe he didn't like me! Maybe that's why he didn't tell me who he was. But I was sure I'd felt some chemistry between us. And what about the roses and sparkler? I was sure Joe was responsible for those. Didn't that mean he liked me? And if he liked me enough to go to the trouble of leaving roses for me, why didn't he come in to the tasting room to see me when he dropped off Clemmie? Maybe he liked me, but he liked Clemmie better when he met her? No, that's crazy thinking. She's beautiful but too young and flighty for him. Maybe he was angry about the police. No, that was an honest mistake on my part. If he didn't tell me the truth about who he was, how was I supposed to know?

I decided not to ask Jillian any more about him. I was just going to have to wait until he came back next month. I guess I still want a little mystery in my life.

* * *

Chapter 9

SPREE

Jillian

"Clemmie, would you consider doing me another favor, as a part-time job?"

"Sure, Jillian, but I live in Bay City, remember, and I have a few more months of school before I graduate." Clemmie looked at me with questioning eyes.

"Oh, this would be in Bay City and you could do it after school or whenever you have free time. My mother lives in Bay City and my sister and I have been worried that she has no family nearby anymore. We want someone who would just check in with her and make sure she is okay and maybe run a few errands for her and do a few chores in her condo. Would you be interested? I know she would like you."

"Wow, is she like in a wheelchair or need diapers changed or anything like that?"

I laughed, "No, just the opposite. She does yoga and dance classes and is in great health. It would just be good for my sister Jackie and me to know that someone is available nearby if she needs anything."

"Cool! Does she like to go shopping? You wouldn't even have to pay me to take her shopping."

"She loves shopping! Her name is Vivian South and I'll write down her address and phone number for you. I'll give her a call and tell her that you'll be calling her. I'll just tell her that you are Chloe's sister and you want to meet her. You don't need to tell her that I'm paying you. Keep track of your time and I'll send you a check every couple of weeks. Does that sound okay?"

"Sounds like the best part-time job ever," Clemmie answered with her glowing smile. "Do you know what time it is in Cancun? I want to call Britney and tell her."

We'd had a very successful day shopping. Clemmie was as good as her word and had hit the shops downtown like a tall, blond whirlwind.

I now had two new bathing suits, with coordinating cover-ups and a pareo, shorts, capris, summer tops, skirts, and a colorful dress and sandals for casual dinners. We had two formal dresses on hold but Clemmie wanted to check the consignment shops before we make a final decision on those. The girl was a wonder. I was actually starting to look forward to this cruise.

We hadn't forgotten Tommy. Chloe picked out a couple of tropical print shirts, a new bathing suit, and some tees for him. We finally stopped for a late lunch and a break at Poppycocks. I ordered a salad. Chloe ordered the lobster ravioli and was eyeing up the desserts in the pastry case. How nice to be seventeen and almost six feet tall.

* * *

Chapter 10

SWEET INTOXICATIONS

Chloe

The book came in the mail on Monday while Clemmie was out shopping with Jillian. I had the day off and I stayed home all day reading it. If I could, I'd include the whole thing here, but that would be plagiarism or copyright stealing or something like that so let me just tell you if you want to read the it, and I highly recommend it, go on Amazon and order a copy for yourself. It's worth it. Skye was right; it's one of the sexiest things I have ever read. I couldn't put it down and I couldn't believe I'd spent an afternoon drinking wine with the author – maybe – if Devlin and Joe were the same person.

Here's the book report version –

Miguel Diablo is a medieval grape farmer turned wine maker in Andalusia, Spain. One year, at harvest season, he seduces Maria Linda, the beautiful daughter of his housekeeper, and convinces her to stomp grapes with him in the moonlight. They make love in the vat infusing the grapes with their passion and adding "the sweet juices of their lovemaking" to the juice of the grapes.

He makes wine from the grapes and bottles it, naming it Maria Linda, and it is wildly successful.

This goes on for several years. Each year Diablo seduces another beautiful woman in the vat of grapes, Blanca, Carmen, Esmeralda, Margarita, and each is honored with her name on the wine.

Diablo's wine becomes well known and highly sought after throughout Spain. Men value it as an aphrodisiac. The King of a neighboring country, who is getting on in years, is having performance problems in the bedroom, if you know what I mean. He sends his most beautiful Courtesan, Teresa, to Diablo to have him name a wine for her. Teresa falls under the spell of the handsome young winemaker and a case of the wine made from the grapes infused with their passion is sent to the King. He is cured and sends for Diablo to personally thank him. During this visit, the young daughter of the King, Princess Clothilde, catches Diablo's eye. He smiles at her and the Princess boldly returns his smile. He asks the King if Princess Clothilde can visit his vineyard at the next harvest to be the inspiration for the next wine.

I'm not going to spoil it for you by telling you the rest of the story. Really, you have to read it for yourself. What is really surprising is that a guy, Devlin Carmichael, a college student from Upstate New York, wrote this.

And, after reading this, how am I going to be able to work with him next month when he comes back to Northern Lights without dragging him into the nearest vat of grapes?

* * *

Chapter 11

DEVLIN'S RETURN

Chloe

Devlin was returning to Northern Lights on the second Thursday in March, the day before Jillian and Tommy were scheduled to fly to Florida for their cruise. I couldn't decide how I felt about meeting him, or meeting him again if he really is the Joe of my private wine party. If he really is Joe, why did he use a fake name, not tell me he was related to Jillian, and pretend not to know about wine? If he is Joe, it would explain how he disappeared that night with no car. He could have simply walked around the corner of the tasting room building and over to the house. I never looked for footprints in the snow going that way.

Even if he is not Joe, I know Devlin wrote *Sweet Intoxications*, which I have now read three times, and I'm not sure about how I feel working with the guy who could imagine and write such steamy sex scenes. I mean, I've always wanted to stomp grapes, but I never imagined having sex in the vat until I read that book. Now it's all I can think about. I just know I'm going to be blushing like crazy every time I look at him.

For the first time since I was fourteen, I'd spent Valentine's Day without a date, home alone in my comfy sweats with take-out coq au vin from Lil's restaurant, a bottle of Chloe Sparkles, and my copy of *Sweet Intoxications*. Lil was working. Summer and Skye both had dates. Mandy was with her husband.

Strangely, I didn't feel badly about being alone. I'd had offers. Summer's cousin was in town and she would have set me up with him. An old friend called out of the blue and asked me out when he discovered I was still single. Even Floyd Dufek wanted to be my Valentine, but I was not interested. I was biding my time, reading, wondering, dreaming and waiting.

I woke up early on that Thursday morning. After all of the waiting and wondering, I came to the conclusion that I really hoped Devlin was Joe. I wanted to see Joe again. And I wanted answers.

The door was already unlocked when I got to Northern Lights. I figured Jillian or Tommy was in early. They had a lot to do before they left on their trip. The fire was roaring in the fireplace and the aroma of fresh coffee competed with the usual yeasty smell of the fermenting wine. I hung up my coat, kicked off my boots, and nearly jumped out of my skin when a voice behind me said "Hello, Chloe."

I turned around. Joe was standing by the door to the office, looking just as good as I remembered. "Hello, Joe," I replied and stepped toward him - right into a puddle of melted snow on the stone tiled floor. I jumped again as the cold water soaked my socks. "Damn it!" I yelled.

Joe looked startled. "Not quite the response I was hoping for," he said, looking in my eyes and not at my wet feet.

"Umm, wet floor, cold feet", I explained holding up my right foot and dripping sock.

Joe crossed the space between us quickly, scooped me up in his arms and carried me to one of the leather chairs by the fireplace. He gently set me down in the chair, put my feet up on the footstool, peeled off my wet socks, and draped them over the fire screen. He sat on the stool, took my cold feet in his warm hands and began rubbing them gently, warming them quickly. I was very glad I had gotten a pedicure on Saturday.

He looked up at me, still rubbing, "Better?" he asked.

"Bliss," I answered and blushed. "Who are you?" I had to know now. "Joe or Devlin?"

"Well," he hesitated, "Both, I guess."

"Multiple personalities?"

"Not exactly," he replied. "My name is Devlin Joseph Carmichael. Sometimes, I just use my middle name, Joe. It's hard to explain, but sometimes people get the wrong impression of me if they know me as Devlin."

"Because of the book?" I asked.

Now it was his turn to blush. "You know about the book? How did you find out?"

"There was a picture of you in the Northern Lights camera. Skye, who works here now, thought she recognized you from the picture on a book back cover, but she couldn't remember the name of the book or the author, so she called her friend Katy who remembered the name of the book but couldn't find her copy because someone had borrowed it and didn't return it so I went to the bookstore, but it was closed, and I couldn't find it on Google, then Clemmie suggested I try Amazon. I found it online and ordered it."

He groaned. "You went to all that trouble to find it? I suppose you've read it?"

My turn to blush again. "Three times," I confessed, imagining us naked in a vat of dusky, sun-warmed, wet, slippery grapes.

* * *

Jillian

"Well, I guess you two have met." Chloe and Devlin hadn't heard me come in to the tasting room. Chloe was lying back in one of the big leather chairs and Devlin was holding her bare feet in his hands. They both turned to me with embarrassed looks on their faces. "What's going on?" I asked.

"Wet socks. Watch out for the puddle," Devlin explained hastily, letting go of Chloe's feet.

"I'm so tired of all this snow. Only one more day and Tommy and I will be out of it and in the Caribbean sunshine. We can't thank you enough, Dev, for coming and helping out so we can get away."

"Consider it my birthday present to you, Aunt Jilly," Devlin replied. But from the way he was looking at Chloe, I thought he had other reasons for coming back to Michigan and Northern Lights.

The door opened behind me, letting in a fresh blast of cold March air, and Tommy made his entrance with Coco at his heels. He was wearing one of his new bright tropical print shirts over a red long-sleeved long-john shirt. Chloe, Devlin and I all burst out laughing.

"Tommy North has morphed into Tommy Bahama!" Chloe was laughing so hard I thought she might fall out of the chair. She was kicking her bare feet in the air, ruby red toenails reflecting the light from the fire.

"You like it?" Tommy flashed his dimples at us. "Clemmie picked it out for me. That girl is one heck of a shopper. She said that Jilly and I are going to be cruise fashionistas. Or Jilly will be and I will be a fashionisto. Is that right? My Spanish is very rusty."

Devlin was cracking up, "All you will need to know is *mas cervasas, por favor.*"

"*Y Margaritas para mi senora linda!*" Tommy added, spinning me around and dipping me over his arm. Coco barked and danced along with us.

"Don't forget the *vino!*" Chloe added.

The door opened again and Mandy came in holding her four year old son, Connor, by the hand. She looked around at Tommy in his crazy outfit dancing me around the room, Chloe in the chair with her bare feet in the air and her socks starting to sizzle on the fire screen, and Devlin sitting next to her looking very cozy and happy.

"Good morning," she said cheerfully. "I hope you don't mind that I brought Connor in for a little while. Ted has an appointment this morning and will pick him up as soon as he is finished." Then she did a double take and stared at Devlin, eyes wide. "Oh my God – are you Joe?"

"Mandy, this is my nephew, Devlin Carmichael. He's going to be helping out here while we're gone."

Mandy glanced at Chloe, "Devlin, not Joe?" she asked.

"Umm, both actually", Chloe answered.

I was getting confused. "Who is Joe?"

Connor ran in to give Chloe a big hug. "Aunt Koee, can I have some wine?" he asked.

"Sure you can, Con-man." Still barefoot, she took him over to the bar and pulled his special wine bottle from the refrigerator.

"Isn't he a bit young for wine?" Devlin asked Chloe. "You might want to check his ID."

"This is special wine for kids," Chloe replied with a wink, taking a plastic glass from the shelf. "Con-man loves it."

"Apple juice in a fancy bottle," Mandy whispered. She looked at Devlin closely. "If you are Devlin, who is Joe?"

"Yes," I echoed. "Who is Joe?"

Devlin groaned and put his face in his hands, shaking his head. He lowered his hands and looked up at us. "I'm Joe. I met Chloe last month when I was here for a few days. I told her my name was Joe. And then she almost had me arrested and I didn't see her again to straighten the whole thing up."

Chloe piped up from the bar. "If you had told me you were Tommy and Jillian's nephew, I wouldn't have called the cops when I saw the Jeep being stolen. I mean, I would have known it was you driving and it wasn't being stolen. So don't blame me for almost getting you arrested."

Connor looked up from his apple juice, "Who's 'rrested? Is the bad man going to jail?"

Chloe hugged him. "No sweetheart, he's not a bad man and nobody's going to jail. Would you like some crackers with your wine?"

Connor nodded and Chloe got out the crackers for him and poured him more juice. "Right, Devlin Joseph? You're not a bad man, just not a truthful one. I even mentioned to you that the Syrah grapes we use in Chloe Sparkles come from your family's vineyard and you didn't say a word. You let me go on and on about our wines and all the time you're the big wine expert from New York. Were you testing me or something?"

Devlin crossed the room to her. "I'm sorry. I saw you and you were so beautiful and I wanted to meet you. I never meant to make you feel bad. It's just that I got the idea from Tommy…"

"Tommy?" I interrupted. They both turned to me. I think they forgot that Tommy, Mandy and I were there listening. "Tommy, what did you do?"

"Me? I didn't do anything. Did I?" Tommy looked surprised.

"Well," Devlin tried to explain. "Remember when we were in the office and I was watching Chloe through the one-way glass?"

"Oh, yeah," Tommy chuckled. "You couldn't take your eyes off her."

"I asked you if she had a boyfriend and you told me about her dating ideas. That she liked mystery. So I took a picture of myself and left it in the camera for her to find. Then while you were out that afternoon, I went to the tasting room knowing that she was there alone. We had a great time together. So much so that when I left, I couldn't tell her I was there under false pretenses. So I just left. But I found a box of sparklers with some old summer decorations in the basement and the next morning I went out very early and bought a rose at Meijer and shoveled out her car and left the rose and sparkler. I was planning on going to see her later and explaining, but then she almost had me arrested and her sister came and Aunt Jilly got home and there just wasn't a chance to see her privately, until this morning. And now you're all here so I guess I have to apologize in public. I'm sorry, Chloe. Please let me take you out to dinner tonight to try to make up for it."

Chloe glanced at Mandy. "It's Thursday, our girl's night," she told Devlin.

Mandy spoke up. "That's okay. I was going to cancel tonight, anyway. Our babysitter has the flu and Ted has a big project due tomorrow and needs to work tonight. Go with Devlin. I'm sure Lil, Summer, and Skye will all understand." She turned to Devlin with a grin. "We've all read the book."

"What book?" Tommy and I both asked, puzzled.

"You don't know about *Sweet Intoxications?*" Chloe asked.

"It's only the sexiest romance novel ever written," Mandy added.

Joe had to confess. "When I was in college, I was dating a girl who was hooked on romance novels. She read them by the dozen and I always teased her about them and laughed at how they were all the same except for the names, locations and hair colors. You know the typical bodice rippers with a picture of Fabio and a half-naked girl on the cover? Well, she resented that, and bet me that I couldn't write anything half as good. I was taking a creative writing class, and Spanish, and the viticulture program so I combined the three and made up this wild story and wrote it just for the bet. Well, she loved it and showed it to her friend who showed to her mother who was an editor with a small publishing house and the crazy thing got published. I should not have let them publish it under my real name, with a picture of me no less. I think every girl in my school, and every girl in upstate New York, bought a copy of it. I had to go undercover. That's why I call myself 'Joe' sometimes when I meet a new girl. I never know if she's read the book. The whole thing got very embarrassing. But it paid my tuition and then some."

Chloe burst out laughing. "Will you autograph my copy, please? At dinner tonight."

"I want a copy to take on the cruise with me", I added.

"Better order it on Amazon right now, with overnight shipping. I'm not parting with my copy, even for a week."

Devlin bent and hit his head on the bar. "You should have sent me to jail!"

"Bad man," Connor said. "You go to jail! No wine for you."

* * *

Chapter 12

DATE NIGHT

Chloe

I left work at five to rush home and get ready for my official first date with Joe, or Devlin. I wasn't sure what to call him. Jillian was minding the store and would take care of closing up. Joe/Devlin had spent the day working with Tommy and I didn't have time to talk to him again all day, except to ask him to pick me up at seven. I called Lil earlier to fill her in. She was okay with cancelling girl's night too, as long as I agreed to take Joe/Devlin to Nokomis for dinner. Since we were cancelling girl's night, she would be cooking and wanted to check him out. She's read the book too.

Nokomis, Daughter of the Moon, is the Bay front restaurant where Lilianna is head chef. The owner, Wenonah, is from Sault Ste. Marie in the Upper Peninsula of Michigan and named the restaurant after her grandmother, Nokomis, who was named after the grandmother of Hiawatha in the Longfellow poem. It's a beautiful place with the best view of Grand Traverse Bay and the best food anywhere.

At home, I ran a bath instead of my usual quick shower, adding jasmine scented oil. As I soaked, I imagined the evening to come. My handsome date would pick me up in…there I was stumped. What was he going to drive? He flew in to Traverse City. Did he rent a car or would he be borrowing Tommy's Jeep? He would be nicely dressed, freshly shaved, and smelling of good cologne. Would he bring me chocolates or flowers? Or both? We would drive through the dark and snowy town to Nokomis where we would be shown to the best table by the window. I had Lil reserve it for us. Candles would be lit. We would study the wine list together. When the wine was ordered and poured, Joe/Devlin would expertly swirl, examine, and taste before approving. He would then gaze adoringly into my eyes and toast our new beginning.

The bath water was cooling and I decided I'd better get out and get dressed so this magical evening I was anticipating could get started. Scrubbed, shaved, buffed, and shampooed, I started pulling clothes from my closet. Too bad it was 25 degrees and windy out. No skin baring sexy dress on this date. I settled on a short black skirt and a lacy white blouse. I'd wear black tights and black leather high-heel boots. I checked the mirror. The blouse was wrong. Remembering Joe's appreciation of Ruby Lips, I opened my hope chest, my cedar chest, where I stored my wool sweaters and pulled out the wine red cashmere v-neck. Much better, soft and subtly sexy. I put on my ruby earrings, a birthday gift from my parents many years ago. Ruby is my birthstone. A long, soft multi-colored scarf draped casually around my neck finished the look. Good.

I checked the time. 6:45. I quickly blew my hair dry and put on my makeup and a spritz of my favorite perfume.

7:00. Now I was getting nervous. I never feel like this before a date. 7:15. Now he's late and I'm getting worried. I poured myself a glass of chardonnay and sat on the kitchen counter so I could watch out of the window that overlooks the parking lot. At 7:25, I saw Tommy's green Jeep pull in. Joe/Devlin got out and headed to the condo entrance. I hopped down from the counter, checked the mirror, straightened my skirt, rearranged my scarf and waited for the doorbell.

"Chloe, I'm so sorry I'm late," Joe/Devlin said as soon as I opened the door. "I had a little accident."

"Oh my God!" I gasped, spotting blood on his leather jacket and mud on his pants and boots. "Are you alright? What happened? Was anyone else hurt?"

Joe/Devlin was shaking his head. "No, nothing like that. I'm okay, but I hit a deer. It jumped right out in front of me and I couldn't stop in time."

"But the blood…"

"Not mine," Joe/Devlin said. "I stopped and tried to pull the deer off the road so no one else would hit it. Bad idea. It wasn't dead, just stunned, bloody and confused. It ran into me, knocking me over, then ran off into the woods. I had to call the cops to get an accident report for Tommy's insurance company. The Jeep is a little banged up in front but still drivable."

I ran cold water over a dishtowel and tried to wipe the blood from his jacket. "Our reservation is for 7:30. I'll just call Nokomis and tell them we'll be a little late."

"Nokomis? As in *By the shining big sea waters*?" Joe/Devlin asked.

"*Stood the wigwam of Nokomis*, *Daughter of the Moon, Nokomis*" I completed the quote. "You're familiar with Hiawatha?" He nodded and I continued. "The owner of the restaurant named it that after her grandmother, who was named after the Nokomis in the poem. My best friend and roommate, Liliana, is head chef there. The food is great!"

I was not helping the jacket much, just smearing the stain around, so I gave it up, got my coat, which Joe/Devlin helped me put on, and we headed out.

"Turn left up here," I told Joe/Devlin as I scrolled through my cell phone for the number for Nokomis. He turned.

"I don't think this is right," he said calmly. "We're going the wrong way on a one-way street."

I looked up from my cell and shrieked at the headlights coming directly at us. "Pull over!" Suddenly, blue flashing lights appeared on the other car and Joe/Devlin was pulling into a parking lot. "I meant turn left at the next light, not here."

The deputy was approaching the Jeep and Joe/Devlin rolled down the window. I peered out. It was Tony, the same officer who responded when I'd reported the Jeep stolen last month, and as it turned out, the same officer who had responded to the Jeep/deer accident earlier this evening.

"Hi, Tony," I spoke up right away. "I'm sorry, it's all my fault. Devlin is from out of state and I was giving him directions. I'm afraid I wasn't very clear on just where to turn."

Tony laughed, "Chloe, you sure seem to be doing your best to get this guy in trouble. First you report that he stole Tommy's Jeep and now you're sending him the wrong way down one-way streets. Where are you headed?"

"We're going to dinner at Nokomis," I answered. Tony turned to Devlin and gave him directions.

"Thank you, Officer," Devlin smiled.

"Yes, thanks, Tony," I added. "Come up to Northern Lights soon. I owe you a bottle of wine."

We made it to Nokomis without further mishap, but when I stepped out of the Jeep I slid on a patch of ice and fell on my butt, breaking the heel of my boot on the way down. It was worth a broken boot because Joe/Devlin scooped me up in his arms again and carried me into the restaurant. I took the opportunity to put my arm around his neck and smell his spicy sweet aftershave. He smelled as good as he looked.

We made quite an entrance, Joe/Devlin in his bloody jacket and muddy pants, carrying me in my wet skirt and my broken boot.

Annie, the hostess, had been watching for us. Lil must have been watching too and she came rushing out of the kitchen. "What happened?" she gasped. "Are you okay?"

"We're fine," I was laughing at their shocked expressions. Joe/Devlin put me down and I limped over to the bench by the door. "Just a broken heel, an injured deer, a bloody jacket, and a dented Jeep. Nothing one of your good dinners and a bottle of wine can't fix."

Lil's attention turned to my date. "So you are Joe, or Devlin? What should we call you, anyway?"

"Have you read the book?" Joe asked her seriously.

"Oh, yeah," Lil answered with a knowing grin.

"Then please call me Joe." He held out his hand to her. "Very nice to meet you. Chloe tells me you're a fantastic cook."

"Chloe's right," Annie said. "Let me help you to your table. Lizzy will be your server tonight."

"I've got an extra pair of Crocs in the kitchen you can wear, I don't know if those boots can be fixed." Lil hurried back to the kitchen and returned a moment later carrying a bright orange pair of rubber clogs. I sat down on the bench and Joe, yes I'll call him Joe, unzipped my boots for me and pulled them off gently.

"These don't go too well with your outfit," he laughed as he slipped the Crocs onto my feet. I didn't care. I was starting to feel like Cinderella. If the Crocs fit…

Annie took us to our table by the window. It was too dark to see the bay, but the city lights circling it twinkled like a diamond necklace around the shoreline. I took a good look at Joe as he looked out the window. With the bloody jacket off, he looked much better. He was wearing a nice green wool sweater that looked great with his dark hair and enhanced the green in his hazel eyes. He turned from the window, smiled at me, and picked up the wine list. "What would you like to drink?" he asked me.

"You choose, please." I was too busy looking at him to look at the wine list.

"I see they have Northern Lights wine here, Shall we support Aunt Jilly and Tommy or try the competition."

"I'm all for supporting Jillian and Tommy, but we can drink that anytime. You really should try some of the other Grand Traverse or Leelanau County wines. The whites are especially good. I like the pinot gris from this place." I pointed to the list. "The rieslings are excellent but most of them are too sweet for me with dinner. We can try them with dessert if you like.

Lizzy came over to take our drink order. Hi, Chloe, nice shoes," she teased. Joe ordered a bottle of the pinot gris and Lizzy listed the night's specials for us.

Joe looked around the room. "This place is beautiful. It reminds me of an old Adirondack lake lodge."

"Then I guess I'd like the Adirondacks because this is one of my favorite places in Traverse City," I replied. It was beautiful, very homey with a field stone fireplace, beamed ceilings, comfortable tables and chairs and booths.

Have you ever been to upstate New York?" Joe asked me.

I shook my head.

"It's a lot like here," Joe described it. "We have hills and big lakes, the Finger Lakes, and lots of vineyards and wineries."

Lizzy brought the wine, opened it with flair and poured a small tasting for Joe. He held it to the light as he examined it, swirled it in his glass to check for legs, held it to his nose to sample the bouquet, and finally took a drink, holding it in his mouth for a moment so the flavor could develop. He swallowed and smiled. "Very nice," he told Lizzy and she poured me a glass and refilled Joe's before leaving us with the menus.

Joe raised his glass to me, "There are five reasons why we should drink: good friends, good wine or feeling dry or lest we should be by and by, or any other reason why."

I don't remember what we ate that night. Sorry Lil, I'm sure it was great, but all of my attention was focused on Joe. We sat by our window, drank our wine, ate our dinners, and talked for hours. Just like our first afternoon together in February, we never seemed to run out of things to talk about. We talked about wine, of course; Joe prefers dry reds, and the weather; Joe likes winter and summer equally, and movies; Joe likes action adventures, and books; Joe likes detective mysteries, and sports; Joe likes to ski in the winter and kayak in the summer. And I discovered that I like learning all I could about Joe. Mysteries are okay for books, but I'd had enough mystery in my dating life and was ready for full disclosure.

Eventually, we got around to discussing our families. Joe had already met Clemmie. "Cute kid", he called her. "I have a brother just a bit older than her. David is in his second year of college."

"Is David going into the winery also?" I asked. "How is it working with your parents? I love my folks, but I don't think I would want to be with them day and night."

"Davy's been working at the winery all of his life, just like I did. It's what we know and what we love, I thought about doing something else, medicine or architecture or driving race cars, but in the end I came back to wine making. I love working the land and creating wines from our harvest. Mom does most of the business side of Wild River, and that's fine with me, Dad and Davy. We'd rather be in the vineyards than in the office with the books. What I'd really like is to have my own winery someday, but I'd need a partner, or two, to do what Mom does." Joe paused. "What about you?" he asked. "When you were a little girl, what did you want to be?"

I laughed, "I wanted to be a princess. I wanted to marry Prince Charming and live in the castle and wear beautiful dresses and a crown covered in sparkly rubies, diamonds and emeralds."

Joe didn't laugh at my dream like so many others had done. "Prince Charming's loss is my gain," he said and raised his glass to me.

I lightly touched his glass to mine. "You don't happen to have a white horse, do you?"

"No, but I know where I can borrow one."

Lizzy chose that moment to come and clear away our dishes and tell us that dessert would be right out.

"But we didn't order dessert," I told her.

"You didn't have to. Lilianna made something special for you."

A moment later she was back with a tray holding two dishes of vanilla ice cream, cherries and a hot pan of cherry liqueur. Lizzy expertly lit the liqueur with a long match and then poured the flambé over the cherries and ice cream. Voila, Cherries Jubilee!

"That's impressive," Joe said as Lizzy served us the elegant dessert. "I've heard of this but never had it before."

"Careful! The sauce is still hot." I warned him, but I was too late. I scooped some ice out of my water glass and held it to the burn on Joe's lower lip.

"Delicious and dangerous!" Joe said when he could talk again. "Just the way I like my food."

"Poor guy," I replace the melted ice with a cold, wet napkin. "First I almost have you arrested, then you get in an accident on the way to pick me up, and now you get burned by dessert. Seems like just being around me is dangerous for you."

"Like *Fatal Attraction?*" Joe grinned. "I'll take my chances, unless I find a rabbit boiling in a pot on the stove. Then I'll get worried." He reached across the table and took my hand. "Think we can run Northern Lights together for a week without blowing the place up?"

I laughed, "As long as we don't flambé the wine we'll do great."

Lil took a break from the kitchen to join us for coffee. "Dinner, okay?" she asked.

"Incredible!" Joe answered "You're even a better cook than my Grandmother. That was the best dinner I've ever had."

"Oooww, wait 'til I see Vivian again. I'm going to tell," I teased.

"You know my grandmother?" Joe was surprised.

"Jillian's mom? Sure, she's been up here to visit several times and likes to help out with the customers in the tasting room. She's a hoot."

"That's for sure. I haven't seen her in a while. Maybe I can get down to Bay City before I head back to New York."

I didn't want to think about Joe going back to New York already. He just got here.

All too soon we said our good-byes and drove back through the dark streets to my condo. For once, we were quiet with each other, but it was a comfortable silence, if you know what I mean. We didn't need to talk.

"Would you like to come in?" I asked when we arrived. His reply was a simple "Yes."

I was still wearing Lil's orange Crocs instead of my broken boots, so Joe held my arm as we walked carefully to the door. We dropped our shoes and jackets by the door and headed into the kitchen. There was a cold bottle of Chloe Sparkles in the fridge. Joe popped the cork while I got the flutes from the cupboard. In the living room, I flipped the switch to turn on the gas fireplace - instant romance. The CD player was preloaded with some of my favorite oldies, the slow, soft romantic ones, of course. We settled into my big, red velvet sofa.

"To my sparkly girl," Joe said as we tinked glassed and drank. He called me "his girl" and it felt right. Joe set his glass on the coffee table. He held his hand out for my glass and I gave it to him. He set mine down next to his. I was in his arms and ready to kiss and be kissed, finally. I'd been waiting for this since February. Our lips met.

"Ouch!" Joe winced and pulled back from me.

"Not quite the response I was hoping for," I said, echoing his words to me when I first saw him this morning. Then I remembered. "Oh, your lip! The burn. I'm sorry."

"Don't apologize. Let's try again."

This time, I restrained myself and kissed him very softly, gently, mindful of the burn on his lip. My hands found their way to his ears, and neck, and into his hair. His lips were soft and warm and he tasted of Cherries Jubilee and champagne. I could have kissed him all night.

Mom, if you are reading this someday, I just want to go on the record by saying that I don't usually bring guys home and make out with them after the first date.

I won't go into the juicy details. Joe's the sexy romance writer, not me. Let's just say, things were progressing nicely until I put a damper on our doings when my right foot brushed across the coffee table, knocking over our half full champagne flutes.

"Watch where you step, Joe" I called as I went to the kitchen for paper towels. "There's broken glass everywhere. We don't need any more bloody accidents tonight."

Ten minutes later, Joe was picking slivers of glass out of my finger. "Let's see, dented Jeep, bloody jacket, broken boot, burned lip, and now a cut finger. Not bad for one evening. Want to do this again sometime? I'll be here all next week." He tenderly wrapped a band aid around my injured finger.

Only a week, I thought to myself. No time to waste. "How about tomorrow?"

"I'm driving Aunt Jilly and Tommy to the airport in the morning, then I'm all yours."

All mine, I liked the sound of that. "I'll be pulling double duty at Northern Lights with Jillian gone, so I won't have much free time, but I think I can squeeze you in."

He grinned and kissed my bandaged finger. "And I'll be busy with testing and bottling, but I have to take coffee breaks and eat lunch, and fill up my lonely evenings. It'll just be me and Coco in the house, all by our lonesome. She's a good kisser but you're better." He touched my lips gently and I almost swooned.

"Goodnight, Chloe. Till tomorrow, then, Princess Sparkles."

I laughed, "Goodnight, Senor Diablo. *Hasta manana.*"

* * *

Cheers to Cherries Port – The perfect blending of red wine, brandy, and Grand Traverse Cherries, aged in new French Oak. Our Cherry Port will warm you, heart and soul on cold winter nights.

Chapter 13

PORT IN A STORM

Chloe

It was snowing again. And it was blowing. And it was very, very cold. From the windows of the tasting room, I couldn't see the house. I hoped that Joe was able to find it in the storm and, even more importantly, that he could find his way back again.

We had sent the crew home several hours ago, just before the State Police issued warnings to stay indoors and off the roads. The power went out about 30 minutes after that.

Joe had struggled out to uncover and start the generator. It would provide just enough power to keep the equipment running and to keep things from freezing. I had built up the fire in the tasting room while Joe went to check on the house and get some food and blankets. We were going to be stuck here for awhile and could cook over the fire. There was plenty to drink.

Normally, I don't like blizzards, but I was happy about this one. We met during a blizzard. It seemed fitting that we would spend the night together for the first time during another blizzard.

Joe and I had been working together all week and had barely had any time alone. We'd been able to have coffee and rolls in the mornings before work started every day. We'd tried to meet for lunch, but couldn't always. Between customers at the tasting room and Joe's work in the vineyards and bottling room, the most we could do was grab a quick sandwich, a hug and a kiss. Evenings were not much better. With the Jeep in the shop for repairs, Joe was limited to Jillian's car, a vintage Jag that he was afraid to drive for fear of hitting another deer. I didn't feel comfortable staying over with Joe in their house or bringing him to the condo while Lil was there.

Now, the crew was gone, no customers would be coming in, and we had the cozy old tasting room to ourselves.

The door blew open and Joe stumbled in. I rushed over to slam the door against the wind and the snow blowing in on the stone floor.

"Are you under there?" I asked as I tried to brush the snow off Joe's hat and coat.

He handed me a pile of blankets. "Better shake off the snow and put these by the fire. We're going to need them later. I found filet mignon and garlic toast in the freezer, and brought dog food for Coco. Tonight we feast."

I laughed and took the blankets. Ummm, filets, wine, dinner by the fire on the blankets with Joe. This storm was a gift from Heaven. And Mom, if you're reading this, I don't normally sleep with guys I've only known for a week, plus one afternoon last month, but everything about my relationship with Joe was different from any other I'd ever had. It's a cliché, I know, but I felt like I'd known him forever. We laughed at the same things and finished each other's sentences.

But, underneath that comfort and familiarity was a sexual attraction that was impossible to ignore. I wanted him and he wanted me. It was that simple. And now we were alone together for the night.

The weather forecast was bad. The storm would continue until sometime tomorrow and we were stranded in the tasting room with only candles for light, the fireplace for heat, steaks to eat, and wine to drink. How perfect.

While Joe was at the house, I had taken the cushions from the chairs and arranged them on the floor near the fire. Coco was curled up on her bed in the corner. Soft music was playing on my ipod. The tray was loaded with a bottle of cherry port, cheese and crackers and two wine glasses. I know, you're supposed to have port after dinner, not before. But it's a great warmer upper and I was chilled to the bone.

"Let's have appetizers while the steaks thaw."

Joe was still pulling off wet clothes. "Be right with you," he said and dropped his jeans. Okay, so he was wearing long johns under his jeans, but it was still sexy to watch him undress.

Over the howling of the wind outside, I heard a snowmobile motor. "Who in the world is that?" I asked, wiping the frost from the window to see. The snowmobile pulled up in front of the tasting room and the driver got off and headed to our door.

"Please tell whoever it is that we are not open for customers," I told Joe, ducking out of sight behind the chairs. I was wearing only my long johns. My clothes had gotten soaked while carrying in firewood and I'd stripped them off and hung them to dry.

The door crashed open letting in another blast of cold wind and swirling snow. The figure in the snowmobile suit stepped in, slammed the door shut behind him, and pulled off his helmet – Floyd Dufek!

He looked at Joe, standing there in his long johns. "Where's Chloe? What are you doing here?" he demanded.

I popped my head up over the back of a chair. "Hi, Floyd. I'm right here and this is Mrs. North's nephew, Joe, umm, I mean, Devlin. He's working here this week."

"I was worried about you, Chloe. I came over to make sure you was okay in the snow."

"That's sweet of you, Floyd, but you can see that I'm fine. You'd better get home so your folks don't worry about you."

"Would you like a glass of wine before you go, Floyd?" Joe asked. "You're a good man to check on Chloe in the storm, but your parents need you at home. I'll make sure Chloe is safe."

Floyd looked doubtfully at Joe, but walked over to the bar for his glass of wine. I wrapped a blanket around myself and dashed behind the bar to find the 'special' wine bottle with apple juice we keep there for Connor. I poured and quickly passed the glass to Floyd. "Better drink up and get going before the snow gets any deeper." The last thing I wanted was for Floyd Dufek to be snowed in overnight with Joe and me.

Floyd looked from Joe to me. I nodded. "One glass of wine, then you'd better hurry home."

It took two glasses of 'wine', but we finally got Floyd out the door and back on his snowmobile. Alone at last. We got comfortable on the cushions and blankets in front of the fire.

"Ummm, great weather we're having," Joe nuzzled my neck. We're going to have to find a way to keep warm all night. Any ideas?"

"Sure, you're going to stay awake to keep stoking the fire while you rub my feet and feed me steak."

"Oh Chloe, you are so beautiful in that sexy outfit. I may have to rub more than your feet." I was wearing thick socks with my long johns and Lil's orange Crocs. They were so comfortable that I never gave them back to her. I spread some cheese on a cracker and fed it to Joe while he opened the port and poured us each a glass.

"To Old Man Winter," Joe toasted.

"And the West Wind," I added and we drank. I closed my eyes and focused on the sensation of warmth spreading through my body.

"I thought it would be fun to read out loud to each other," I said as I reached behind me and pulled the book out from under the chair where I had stashed it earlier.

"Ghost stories? Like the one about a guy and girl stranded in a haunted old stable during a blizzard," Joe asked.

"Better. I have here an autographed copy of the sexiest romance novel ever written by a college student from New York."

Joe grabbed the book away from me. "Not that, anything but that! Snuggle up here with me and I'll tell you my ghost story. But you'll have to stay very close 'cause it's a very scary story."

I leaned back against Joe's chest. He wrapped his arms and legs around me. "Whooooooo," he moaned like a ghost in my ear. "Long ago in this very stable, lived an old horse named Nightmare, and his groom, Harvey."

"Harvey? That's not a very scary name!"

"Quiet – it's my story, I get to make up the names."

"One dark night while Harvey was sleeping, a bat swooped down from the hay loft and bit Nightmare in the neck." Joe demonstrated by quickly nipping my neck."

"Eeeeeee!" I jumped, startled, and spilled my wine, and Joe's, all over our long johns. "I hate bats."

"How do you feel about spiders?" Joe laughed and tickled me, making his fingers feel like eight legged spiders crawling on me. We were both laughing and rolling on the floor in our red wine splattered long underwear. I tried to grab Joe's hands but he was too fast for me. He got my hands trapped and pinned me to the floor. We stopped laughing suddenly and looked deeply into each other's eyes.

"Chloe," Joe said my name softly. "I think it's time for you to start calling me Devlin." His eyes gleamed green in the firelight.

"Devlin," I whispered, using his first name for the first time. It sounded much sexier than Joe. If my hands had been free, I would have pulled his face down to mine and kissed him. Every nerve ending in my body was aware of his body stretched full length over mine. I wanted him, badly. I'd never been more sure of anything in my life.

Slowly, Devlin lowered his face to mine and kissed me, very softly, barely touching my lips with his. I was melting into the floor. My very bones were dissolving.

Devlin released his grip on my hands and I ran them along the length of his back from his neck, down his spine, then grasped his firm butt with both of my hands and pulled him to me. I wanted him. Did I say that already?

Devlin's hands were warm as he slipped them under my long john top and found my breasts. I arched my back in pleasure when he unhooked my bra and softly cupped my breasts in his hands, teasing my nipples just enough to make me moan with the ache of wanting more.

Devlin raised his head from mine and looked into my eyes. "Are you sure?" he asked me. "I'm sure," I whispered and I stripped his shirt off over his head and ran my hands over his broad, smoothly muscled chest, admiring the gleam of his skin in the firefight. Then I pulled him to me and kissed him deeply.

The wind howled outside, but we were oblivious to the blizzard now. Our universe had shrunk to the cushions and blankets in front of the fire in the old stable. The only witness to our passion was Coco, and she was snoring in her corner.

My top came off next. I'm not sure which of us pulled it off. Maybe we did it together. I untangled myself from my bra and flung it aside. The fire flared suddenly. We both turned to look.

"Oh, my God," Devlin laughed. "Did you just throw your bra on the fire?"

"I don't need it right now," I answered, laughing with him. I guided his hands back to my breasts, showing him how I liked to be touched.

"Ummmm, I like you better without it. You are so beautiful," he murmured as his kissed his way down my neck and across my collarbone.

I slipped my hands under the waistband of his long johns and explored the taut muscles and soft skin I found there. Devlin was moaning softly now and quivering with excitement. I was just starting to ease his pants down his hips when a blast of cold air hit us as the door slammed open and all the candles blew out.

Coco woke up and started barking.

* * *

Life is a Cabernet – There's nothing like a great big cabernet with a steak and this is a great big cabernet. Deep plum, almost purple in color, with complex flavors of raspberries, coffee, pepper, black licorice, dark chocolate and real vanilla. A wine to sink your teeth into. A wine as complex as life itself.

Chapter 14

TO LIFE!

Chloe

"Devlin, are you in here?"

The door slammed shut against the blizzard and Devlin popped his head up like a prairie dog.

"Grandma? What are you doing here?"

Grandma? Vivian? What in the hell was she doing here? I scrambled to find my top and yank Devlin's pants back up.

"Hi, Devlin!" said a second voice. Oh, my God. Was that Clemmie with her? What was going on? I peeked around the chair as I pulled my top back on – minus the bra.

"Do you smell rubber burning?" Clemmie asked.

Vivian was flipping the light switch. "Oh my. Is the power out?"

"Yes, Grandma. The power is out. Let me get the candles relit so we can see. How on earth did you get here?"

"Clemmie drove me up. Jillian told me you were here and I wanted to see you."

Devlin had regained some of his composure and most of his clothes. "There's a blizzard going on and the police have warned people to stay off the roads. Don't you listen to the radio?"

"No, we had a book on tape – *The Sweet Potato Queen's Field Guide to Men*. We laughed all the way here."

I had to come out of hiding sooner or later. Might as well do it now. "Hello, Vivian. Nice to see you again. Clemmie, does Mom know you were driving up here?"

Vivian looked surprised to see me. "Why, Chloe! You're here too? Oh, are we interrupting something?" She seemed to suddenly notice the nest of cushions and blankets by the fire and the tray with wine, cheese and crackers.

Clemmie had noticed. "Chloe Louise! What is going on here? Are we interrupting?" She was laughing. I could have killed her. "Yes, Mom knows, but I'd better call her and let her know we made it okay. The roads were a little slippery but Vivian's got a great big Cadillac and we had no problem." She pulled her cell phone from her pocket and walked over to the fireplace for light.

"What is this?" Clemmie held up the smoking remains of my bra on the end of the fire poker. "I thought I smelled rubber burning. I've got to call Brittany. She'll never believe this."

Devlin looked at me. "Chloe Louise? Is that your middle name?"

"For my paternal Grandmother, but is that important now?" Devlin caught the frustration in my voice, and so, I'm afraid, did Vivian.

"Oh, I'm so sorry. Maybe we should have called first. You young people were having a romantic evening before we came barging in. Clemmie and I can go to the house for the night and you can continue what you were doing."

Could this get any more embarrassing? Things like this usually only happened in those romance novels that Devlin made fun of, not to me.

"Grandma, don't be silly. The house is cold and dark. We have the fire here to keep us warm. We have to stay in here to keep the equipment for the winery running. We were just about to grill some steaks for dinner. We have plenty for all of us. And wine, we have lots of wine."

We were going to need lots of wine to get through this night.

Vivian was hugging Devlin. "I brought a whole cooler full of food for you, including your favorite – cherry pie. Clemmie and I will just run out and bring it in."

"Stay here, Grandma. I'll go."

Clemmie handed him the keys with a sweet smile. "I'll go too and help you with our bags."

Now that the candles were relit, Vivian got a good look at us. "Are you two in your underwear and what is all that red stain?"

"We're wearing long johns. Our clothes got soaked bringing in fire wood. And this is red wine – Cherry Port. Devlin tickled me and I spilled," I tried to distract her. "Vivian, why don't you come and sit by the fire? You must be freezing." I picked up cushions from the floor and put them back in a chair. I spotted my copy of *Sweet Intoxications* and nudged it back under the chair with my foot before she saw it. "Would you like a glass of wine?"

"That would be lovely, dear. I'll have the cabernet, please, if we're having steaks for dinner." She settled herself in the chair. Coco sat next to her and put her head on Vivian's lap to be petted.

I opened a bottle of Life and poured her a big glass. Devlin and Clemmie came back in with another arctic blast, loaded with Vivian's suitcase, Clemmie's bulging backpack, and the cooler full of food. At least we had lots of food.

"I'm thirsty, too," Clemmie called to me so I poured another glass for her. What the heck, she wasn't going anywhere tonight and, with luck, I could get her and Vivian both drunk enough to pass out.

I have to admit, it did turn into a fun night after all. Devlin grilled the steaks perfectly over the fire on makeshift grates from the bottling room. Clemmie and I toasted the garlic bread on long marshmallow forks. From her cooler, Vivian produced homemade potato soup, broccoli salad, fruit salad, chocolate chip cookies, fudge and her famous cherry pie. "All of Devlin's favorites," she told us. We found an old cast iron pot and heated the soup over the fire and drank it out of coffee mugs. Coco supplemented her dog food with the few bites of steak that we offered her. We washed it all down with bottles of Tommy's wonderful Northern Lights cabernet. How many bottles? I lost count. That's Life!

Vivian kept us entertained with stories of Jillian and her sister Jackie when they were little girls. "What about Devlin?" Clemmie asked, making googley eyes at him. She could barely focus. "I'll bet he was a cute little boy."

"Oh, yes, the cutest little guy you can imagine, all curly dark hair and big hazel eyes. But he was a little devil, into everything - including the wine. Dan and Jackie couldn't turn their backs on him for a second or he'd be drinking wine right from the bottles."

"I still like drinking from the bottles," Devlin demonstrated by finishing a bottle of Life. He grinned and wiped his lips with his sleeve. I wanted to lick the wine from his lips.

I did sleep with Devlin that night. The two of us were stretched out on the floor in front of the fire, with Vivian on Devlin's other side, Clemmie on my other side. Coco cuddled up next to Clemmie, and the blizzard howled all around the old stable.

* * *

Chapter 15

THE MORNING AFTER

Chloe

Early the next morning, I woke up to find Devlin lying on his side next to me, watching me quietly. When he saw my eyes open, he put his finger to his lips to tell me to stay quiet. Vivian and Clemmie were still sleeping. Vivian was snoring.

Devlin moved his finger from his lips to mine and I smiled. Ever so quietly he eased forward toward me and kissed me softly. The fire had burned low and my feet were freezing, but the rest of me was burning. He looked so cute with his sleep tousled hair and morning stubble and I'd had some pretty erotic dreams featuring the two of us, just Devlin and me. If it weren't for the sound of Vivian's snoring, I might have forgotten that she and Clemmie were there.

Devlin's finger moved down my neck across my collarbone and slowly traced the shape of my breast through my long john shirt.

Silently, I eased my hand to Devlin's waistband and slipped a finger underneath. Two could play at this game. Our hands were out of sight under a blanket, but our breathing was getting louder and we were both starting to tremble.

Devlin was kissing me again, and blowing in my ear and licking my face, all at the same time! How was he doing that? My eyes flew open. Coco was standing over us busily licking me. A very weird ménage a trois. The day was getting off to a good start.

"I think Coco has to go out," I whispered to Devlin.

"Me, too," Devlin whispered back and kissed me quickly one more time before sliding out of the blankets and into his boots and coat.

I had to pee too, but tried not to think about it. Three women using the bathroom with only melted snow available to flush the toilet created a problem. Devlin and Coco had been going outside. He grabbed a bucket on his way out the door to fill with snow. It takes a lot of melted snow to flush a toilet.

The power was still out. No running water meant no coffee this morning. We had nothing here to drink but wine and a bottle of Connor's apple juice. But there was cherry pie for breakfast!

I snuggled down under the blankets between Clemmie and Vivian and waited for Devlin to come back. As long as he was up, I was sure he would stoke the fire.

It was Saturday morning. Jillian and Tommy were due back this afternoon. Devlin was flying home. Unless the storm continued and the airport closed, I was out of alone time with Devlin.

The snow ended mid-morning and the sun came out. So did the snowplows. The power came back on at noon.

Devlin left for the airport at three o'clock. Jillian and Tommy's plane came in at four and Devlin flew out at five.

Our week was over.

* * *

Jillian

From the hot, blue Caribbean to the frozen, white northland in 24 hours. Last night, we'd had our final dinner aboard our ship, the Neptune. This morning, we'd woken at the port in Fort Lauderdale. Now we were making our final approach to Cherry Capital Airport and the view from the airplane windows was dazzling, blinding white snow and deep blue lakes under a blazing blue sky. Home.

Tommy took my hand, gave me a quick kiss, and asked, "Glad to be back?"

I nodded, smiling at him. "The trip was great. It was the perfect birthday present. You knew just what I needed. Thank you!"

Despite my misgivings and apprehensions, the trip had been just what I needed. Sure, the sun had been hot – Tommy had the tan to show just how hot – but strangely my hot flashes had not seemed so intense. Maybe it was because I had spent every possible moment in the water.

On every island from Aruba to St. Thomas, I'd skipped the tour busses and gone to the beaches to swim in the incredible clear sea. The resort hotels along the beaches had great pools and I'd walked up from the beach to go for dips in several of those also. Nobody checks to see if you are a registered guest at the hotel. On board ship, my favorite spot was the pool. Tommy teased me and said I was going to grow gills, or a mermaid tail, before the trip was over.

The ship was a floating luxury hotel. The food was fabulous. The service was impeccable. The wine list was amazing, even if it didn't include any Michigan wines. We'd met interesting people from around the world. We'd slept like babies, rocked to sleep by the rhythm of the waves after dancing on the ship's decks in the moonlight.

Devlin was at the airport to meet us. One look at him and I knew something was up. Before I could ask, he was greeting us with hugs and a kiss for me and a manly handshake for Tommy.

"Welcome back to the cold and the snow. We had a blizzard yesterday that knocked out the power overnight. Everything's fine, though. No damage. How was your trip?"

"The trip was great. We had a wonderful time," I replied. "We can't thank you enough for taking over for us so we could go. How did you and Chloe get along working together all week?"

The smile on his face was all the answer I needed. "That good, huh? I'm glad! Chloe is a wonderful girl. I knew you two would be good together."

"When do you want to take another vacation? I'll come back anytime. I wish I didn't have to leave now, but Dad needs me at Wild River."

Devlin helped us collect our bags and get them to the car. We were still dressed in tropical clothes, but Chloe had remembered to send our winter coats with Devlin and we put them on gladly. Northern Michigan in March can be warm as a balmy spring day or as cold as deepest winter. Today the sun seemed to shine as brightly as it had in the Caribbean, but the air was Arctic cold and the coats felt wonderful.

"My flight will be boarding in a few minutes. I'd better go." Devlin hugged me again. "Bye, Aunt Jilly, Uncle Tommy." He turned to go, then turned back. "Oh, I almost forgot. Grandma's at your house. She and Clemmie showed up last night with a cooler full of food. We all stayed in the tasting room to keep the generator going and slept by the fireplace, Coco too. Grandma snores!"

Devlin was laughing, but I could just imagine what his plans for the evening with Chloe had been before Mom and Chloe's little sister showed up. Mom had always had a sense of when her daughters needed extra chaperoning and now, it seemed, her grandson too. But at age 29, I thought he was entitled to a night with a woman without his grandmother butting in.

* * *

White Water – Summer sunshine in a bottle. The unique blend of Chardonnay, Reisling, Pinot Gris and native New York Catawba grapes produces summer flavors -strawberries, rhubarb, grass, green apples, and lemons. Crisp and dry and refreshing. The perfect libation after running the rapids.

Chapter 16

WHITE WATER

Chloe

Absence doesn't make the heart grow fonder. It makes the heart grow lonelier.

Ever since Devlin flew back to New York, he is all I have thought about. We talked on the phone at least twice a day and e-mailed or texted each other all the time. I lived for the sound of his voice on the phone or the words that he typed to me. Good thing we both have unlimited minutes and texting on our cell phone plans.

We'd tried several times to arrange to meet, but something always got in the way. One weekend, I went to Bay City for my parent's anniversary party – 35 years together. The next weekend Devlin had to go to a winemakers' conference. Then Lil and I had fittings for our dresses and bunches of other stuff to do for the wedding. Next he caught a bad cold and spent a weekend in bed coughing and blowing his nose.

It seemed crazy, since we really had spent so little time together and hadn't known each other for very long, but I couldn't stand being separated from him. Maybe if our one night together hadn't been interrupted by his grandmother and my little sister, I wouldn't feel the need to be with him again so urgently. Maybe it's unrequited lust that makes the heart grow fonder. Whatever it was, by the end of April, I was desperate to do something about it.

I went on-line and found a flight from Traverse City to New York and booked a seat. On Friday, I was going to fly to his arms via Delta Airlines. I didn't tell Devlin. I was going to surprise him.

I took the weekend off work. Jillian encouraged me to go. She would cover for me at Northern Lights. Skye was working with her. Mandy would be available if they got really busy. Devlin had told me that he didn't have any plans for the weekend, just work. I would fly to Ithaca, rent a car, and drive to Wild River. I couldn't wait.

Wild River is between two of the Finger Lakes, Seneca and Cayuga, on the western shore of Cayuga Lake, near the small town of Interlaken. Friday morning, I boarded a flight and flew from Traverse City to Detroit, then to Ithaca. I got a rental car, punched the address into my GPS, and headed north on 89.

It was a beautiful spring day and the drive over the hills between the lakes was breathtaking. This was wine country. Devlin was right - the Finger Lakes region was very much like northwestern lower Michigan. Fruit trees were blossoming, lilacs were blooming, and daffodils and tulips brightened gardens everywhere.

Only 30 miles to go and now I was getting nervous. Would Devlin be happy to see me? Maybe I should have told him, or asked him, about coming to see him. What if he had a girlfriend here? No, that was not possible. We spend all of our free time on the phone. He wouldn't have time for a girlfriend.

I passed three other wineries before I saw the sign for Wild River. I turned down a lane winding through vine covered hills. At the end of the lane was a picturesque building in the style of an old lakeside lodge. Beyond the building, I caught a glimpse of Cayuga Lake gleaming like polished aluminum in the late afternoon sunlight. There were half a dozen cars in the parking lot and there, loading a case of wine into one of them, was Devlin.

I pulled my car into the last spot and stepped out. He was talking to an elderly woman and didn't see me as I quietly walked up behind him. I waited while he opened the door for her and helped her into her car.

"Surprise!" I whispered quietly into his ear and wrapped my arms around him. I felt him jump and turn toward me and quickly kissed him with all the pent up passion of the past month.

"Nice surprise," he said. "Who are you?"

"Very funny, Devlin," I leaned back to look up into his eyes. Those sexy hazel eyes, but somehow different.

"Oh, my God! You're not Devlin! Who are you?"

He looked just like Devlin, but 10 years younger. Was that airplane a time machine or something?

He laughed. "I'm David, Devlin's brother. I guess we look kind of alike. Are you a friend of Devlin's? Duh, stupid question. I guess you must be a good friend, from the way you kissed me."

David grinned and I blushed. "I'm sorry. I thought you were him. I'm Chloe Applewhite. Is Devlin here?"

"Chloe? From Traverse City? You work for Aunt Jilly and Uncle Tommy, right? Devlin's been talking about you non-stop for months."

I nodded, glad to hear that Devlin had told them about me.

"Devlin's gone this weekend," David told me.

"Gone? Gone where?"

"I thought he went to see you. He flew back to Michigan this morning."

My heart sank and legs got wobbly. So much for my surprise. Seems he had the same idea.

David was looking at me with concern. "You'd better come inside and sit down." He took my arm and led me toward the door. "I think you could use a glass of wine."

A dark haired woman in her 50's was pouring wine for customers at the counter. I knew immediately that she must be Jillian's sister, Jackie. She glanced up as David led me to an empty stool.

"Mom," he said. "Meet Chloe."

"Chloe? Devlin's Chloe? What are you doing here?" she stopped suddenly. "Oh, that didn't sound very nice. I'm happy to meet you, but just surprised. Wasn't Dev going to Traverse to see you?"

"I didn't know. I wanted to surprise him so I flew here today and now he's gone."

"She grabbed me and kissed me in the parking lot," David told her with a grin so like his brother's that I could have kissed him again if I weren't so embarrassed. "I thought at first she was one of his groupies."

"I thought he was Devlin," I explained. "What groupies? Devlin has groupies?"

She swatted playfully at David with a bar towel. "No groupies, Chloe. Don't mind him. And don't mind about the mix up. Happens all the time," Jackie said. "Not the kissing, but the confusion. If they weren't ten years apart they could be identical twins. Anyway, Chloe, I'm glad to meet you. I'm Jackie. I've heard a lot about you from Jillian and Devlin both. And now, I think you could use a drink."

She poured me a generous glass of white wine and I drank. The fresh taste of a pure summer's day filled my mouth. I closed my eyes and focused on the complex flavors of strawberries, rhubarb, grass, green apples, and just a touch of lemon. The wine was crisp and dry and utterly refreshing.

Jackie was watching me. "Like it?" she asked.

I nodded. "It's wonderful!"

"It's Devlin's favorite and our bestseller. He developed it himself a few years ago. He named it White Water for the rapids on the river."

The phone behind the counter rang and David went to answer it. "Wild River Winery, Hey Devlin! You'll never guess who's here! Yeah, how'd you know?" David paused, listening. "That's wild! She's really cute and a good kisser, too! What? You want to talk to her, she's right here with Mom."

He handed me the phone. "I wanted to surprise you. I didn't mean to kiss your brother, I thought he was you." The customers at the counter were listening and I blushed again. "They look just alike," I tried to explain.

"I just missed you so much, I had to come. I guess it was stupid to not tell you. Now I'm here and you're there."

"Stay there and I'll fly back," we both said at the same time and laughed. Then I said quickly "I've got a return ticket for Sunday night. Let me see if I can exchange it for tonight, okay? I'll call right now and call you back. Maybe we can salvage part of the weekend, anyway."

I called the airline and after holding for twenty minutes learned that there was only one flight from here to there between now and my flight on Sunday and it was fully booked. No way for me to get back sooner unless I drove. I checked a map. The best way to drive back to Traverse was through Ontario, Canada, and I didn't have my passport with me. I called Devlin back and told him.

When he checked on exchanging his ticket, he had the same problem. We were stuck.

I hung up the phone and turned to Jackie. "I guess I'm here for the weekend. Is there a hotel nearby?"

"Nonsense," she said, "You'll stay here with us. Or better yet, why don't you stay in Devlin's house? It's just across the vineyard and very nice. David can take over for me here. I'll get the key and show you the way. Then you'll join us for dinner tonight and tomorrow we can find something fun to do. Devlin said you've never been to New York before and I'd love to show you around. I know you'd rather do it with Devlin, but we can have a girl's day and have some fun."

"Thank you, Jackie," I said as she got the key and we headed out the door. "That sounds great."

Back in my car, I followed Jackie back up the lane and about a mile down the road. Devlin's house, a Craftsman style bungalow, was small and perfect. "He bought the property and built the house right after college," Jackie told me when we got out of our cars in the driveway. "He, umm, came into some money and wanted to invest it in a place of his own."

"It's okay, I know about the book."

"He told you?" Jackie looked surprised.

"No," I laughed. "It's kind of a long story, but a friend of mine had read it and recognized him from the picture on the back cover, I found it on Amazon and ordered it. And read it - three times. I got him to autograph it for me."

Jackie laughed. "Dev was so embarrassed by the attention he got from that book. I think every girl around here was after him. He started calling himself Joe and even tried dying his hair blond, but they found him. It was great for business. We were swamped with *Sweet Intoxications* fans. Except many of them were too young to drink or buy wine.

A wide front porch with an inviting old-fashioned porch swing led to a welcoming front door. Inside, an open staircase went up to a loft area on the second floor. To the right, wide-planked hardwood floors gleamed under a dark brown leather sofa and chair. A Navaho patterned rug defined the seating area and added a colorful touch of reds and greens. The fireplace was fieldstone with a rough hewn wooden mantle. Hanging over the fireplace was a painting framed in birch bark. In the painting, two black bears were holding red canoe paddles and standing in front of a river. Heavy beams that looked like they came out of an old barn supported the high ceilings. Beyond the sitting area, a round dining table with comfortable looking chairs sat under a rustic chandelier. Four wooden stools were pulled up to a bar which separated the dining area from the kitchen.

In the large kitchen, Mission style cabinets, granite countertops, and stainless steel appliances made me think that Devlin might be a serious cook. French doors opened to a large deck with a grill, table and chairs for outdoor dining, and two Adirondack chairs positioned to take in the beautiful view of vineyard covered hills.

To the left of the staircase, another set of French doors opened to a cozy den. Bookcases lined the wall opposite the windows. A neat desk held a laptop, printer, and a Tiffany style desk lamp. A well-used old overstuffed chair and ottoman were pulled up next to the window.

I carried my bag and followed Jackie up the wide staircase. The loft overlooked the living and dining areas and the bedroom suite filled the rest of the second floor.

So, here I was, in Devlin's bedroom, just me and his mother. Our first romantic night alone together was derailed when his grandmother and my little sister showed up. Now, the romantic weekend I had planned would be spent with his parents and little brother. Is this the revenge of the romance writers? Devlin and I had both made fun of typical romance novels, the boy meets girl and they have lots of obstacles and misunderstandings in the way of true love. We're not like that. How can this be happening to us?

"The bathroom is through here," Jackie was saying, "There are plenty of clean towels. There's room in the closet if you want to hang anything up. I'll turn the heat up for you. Just make yourself at home. Relax for a while and come by about 6:30. We'll have a glass of wine before dinner and you can meet Dan."

"Thank you, Jackie," I said to her. "This is very nice of you. I feel pretty dumb for not telling Devlin I was coming."

"Don't," she replied kindly. "Remember, Dev did exactly the same thing. You two must be perfect for each other. You seem to think just alike. I never did believe that line about opposites attracting."

She left me the key and headed back down the road to the winery. I had a couple of hours to kill before I was due at their house for dinner. I opened my bag and sighed at the sight of the sexy lingerie I had packed. Wouldn't be needing that tonight. I took my toothbrush and toiletries into Devlin's bathroom. Like the kitchen, it had simple Mission style cabinets and a granite counter top. There was a jetted spa tub and a big walk-in shower.

Next, I checked out his closet. The jeans, t-shirts, and sweatshirts hanging there barely took up a third of the big space. Another rod held his dress clothes. I found some empty hangers and added the few items I had packed. They looked nice hanging there in his closet, right at home.

Yeah sure, right at home. I hadn't even slept with this guy yet and here I was practically moving into his house and his family while he was away.

I stretched out on his king size four-poster bed and buried my nose in his pillows, inhaling the faint scent of him left behind. Tears of frustration burned my eyes. I'd been dreaming about this moment but, in my dreams, Devlin was here with me. I ripped off my clothes and tore back the goose down comforter. I rolled in the sheets like a dog, like a bitch in heat, leaving my scent there with his. I should have packed a vibrator.

Later, I put on one of Devlin's t-shirts and went down to the kitchen. I found a bottle of White Water in the refrigerator, a corkscrew and a wine glass, and took them all back upstairs to the bathroom.

A glass of wine and a hot bath in that big tub was just what I needed before dinner with Devin's family.

Jackie and Dan's house was a big old farmhouse, much like Jillian and Tommy's, near the winery. Jackie had pointed it out to me on the way to Devlin's house. I got back in my rental car and drove, carefully, back down the road. I'm embarrassed to report that I drank at least half the bottle of White Water while I was in the bath tub.

David met me at the door. "I have to warn you about my Dad," he whispered. "Don't be fooled again and kiss him."

"What? Why would I do that?" I was confused. Then I saw him. For a second I though Devlin had been able to fly home after all and my heart leapt. It actually did. I always thought that was a silly phrase, but turns out it can happen.

The man walking towards me with a big smile had Devlin's hazel eyes and slightly curling dark hair. It was the fine laugh lines around his eyes and the sprinkling of silver in his dark hair that saved me from throwing myself into his arms. That, and David's warning. How could all three of them look so much alike?

"Hello Chloe. Welcome to New York and Wild River, I'm Dan." He took my hands in both of his and smiled at me. "I'm sorry Devlin isn't here, but I hope we can make up for it." I was hoping that George Clooney is available to play Dan when the movie of my life is made.

His smile was so much like Devlin's that for a moment I was flustered. But the warm welcome and the great aromas coming from the kitchen made me feel right at home.

"I hope you like spaghetti?" Jackie asked when Dan led me down the hall into the big country kitchen. She was stirring pots on the stove, wearing a big apron over her clothes. Her dark hair was tied up in a loose bun at the nape of her neck.

"Love it, but I hope you didn't go to a lot a trouble", I said

"No trouble at all. I make big vats of sauce when I have time and freeze it for quick dinners. Dan made a salad and David did the garlic toast. All I had to do was boil the pasta."

"It smells wonderful! What can I do to help?"

Jackie didn't hesitate. "You can set the table," she told me. "Plates are in that cupboard and silverware in the drawer beneath it." And that simply, I went from feeling like an unexpected guest to a member of a warm, loving family. I found the dishes, silverware, added napkins and wine glasses, and set the big table for our dinner.

Dan opened a bottle of chianti. "We don't always drink our own wines here. Gotta have this with Italian," he explained.

The wine was perfect. The dinner was great. The company was even better. The music coming from the CD player was even great. I found myself humming along to Crosby, Stills, Nash and Young.

David was watching me. "You know this music?"

"Sure, my mom plays it all the time."

"We're still having Woodstock around here," David laughed. "Mom and Dad still think they're there."

"You were at Woodstock?" I was impressed.

"We met at Woodstock," Jackie replied, gazing at her handsome husband over her wine glass.

"She was the most beautiful girl there," Dan added.

"And he was so handsome, this tall man standing in that muddy field with long, wavy dark hair and those beautiful hazel eyes. It was love at first sight for me. I don't know what he saw in me. I hadn't had a bath or a change of clothes in days. I'd lost my hairbrush and my hair was a wild tangled mess. But somehow it didn't matter to him."

"She had lost track of her friends and was wet and cold and hungry. She was irresistible." The way Dan looked at her I knew she was still irresistible to him.

"I've heard this story before," David added. "Personally, I think it was the wet t-shirt and the 60's no bra thing that caught his eye."

Jackie laughed good-naturedly at her younger son. "The only reason I got to go was because my friend, Jody, had an older sister who was going with a bunch of girlfriends and they needed more gas money. We pooled our money and seven of us jumped into an old van with no back seats and headed to New York. We had a box of crackers, a jar of peanut butter, a package of Oreo cookies, and a case of warm Coke. It was a great adventure, but I'd kill my kids if they ever did something like that. When we got back, Jody and I were both grounded for the rest of the summer, but it was worth it."

"And of course, you saw Dan again?" I asked.

"Not for four long months. He came to Michigan at Christmas break. But we wrote letters every week and he called me on Sundays. Long distance phone calls were very expensive then."

"I was saving money for a ring," Dan added. "I asked her to marry me and she said yes. Our parents were against it. We had only known each other for a few months, but we were sure and got married in June."

Jackie continued the story. "We rented a little cabin in the middle of nowhere and tried to farm. We had a goat, a few chickens, and a great big mutt of a dog."

"They named the dog Bobby McGee," David added.

"No, that was a later dog. The first dog we called Woody, short for Woodstock," Dan corrected.

"Bobby was one of Woody's puppies," Jackie added. "Remember that female Labrador the neighbors had?" she asked Dan. "Woody visited there a lot and she had several litters of funny looking pups. Bobby McGee was one of them. Janis Joplin did that song after Woodstock."

"How long did you stay on the farm?" I asked.

"We stuck it out of couple of years, until Dan fell off the barn roof and broke his arm. We had no insurance and no help."

"And no money," Dan added. "We packed up our dog, our record player and our collection of LPs and moved in with my parents until my arm healed. Then I found a job at a winery, Jackie went back to school, and eventually we opened Wild River."

"And they still play that old music," David said with a grin.

I sighed. "That is so romantic!"

Jackie and Dan gazed at each other over their wine glasses remembering that first meeting at the music festival all those years ago. Crosby, Stills, Nash and Young sang *Suite Judy Blue Eyes* and David smiled at me, rolling his eyes at his sentimental parents.

"How did you and Dev meet?" David asked me, breaking the spell.

"Oh, that story is not nearly as good as meeting at Woodstock." I was trying to avoid telling them the whole confused tale. "Tell me about Jillian and Tommy. How did they meet?"

Jackie answered, "When Jillian was in college, her roommate's name was Debbie Easton. Debbie was dating a boy whose last name was something like Weston or Westerling, I forget now exactly what it was, but Debbie thought it would be fun to find a guy for Jillian whose last name was North or Northern."

I must have looked puzzled because she explained, "Our maiden name was South."

I laughed, "I didn't know that. So Debbie found Tommy North for Jillian?"

"Yeah, she looked in the student directory and there he was, Thomas North. So she called him and arranged a blind double date with her roommate, Jillian South."

"And was it love at first sight and happily ever after for them?" I asked getting caught up in the story.

"Not exactly. Debbie took one look at Tommy, dropped Westerling or Westerly or whatever his name was and went after Tommy. Jillian had met a guy in one of her classes that she liked and wasn't really interested in Tommy and Tommy had a girlfriend back home.

"It wasn't until much later that they ran into each other again – at a party we had to celebrate our starting Wild River!"

Dan interjected. "Tommy was there with my sister Amy."

"Uncle Tommy and Aunt Amy!" David said. "I never heard this story before."

"Until he saw Jillian again," Jackie took up the story. "She came from Michigan to help us out with the new business. They remembered each other from Debbie's attempt at a fix up. A week later, Tommy broke up with Amy and called us to ask for Jillian's number." Jackie laughed. "I didn't think Amy was ever going to forgive me, but she did, when she met Harry, who turned out to be the perfect husband for her."

"Anyway, Tommy called Jillian, she went out with him, and they have been together ever since. I guess you could call it love at second sight."

"What a great story!" I turned to David. "Okay, David, your turn. You must have a girlfriend, or two, how did you meet?"

"Beautiful girls just throw themselves at my feet, begging to be kissed," he said jokingly. "No special girlfriend, right now, so if you have a sister, I'm ready, willing, and available!"

"As a matter of fact, I do have a sister. Her name is Clementine and she just turned eighteen. She's so beautiful, she has boys throwing themselves at her feet, begging to be kissed. I think she might like you."

"Clementine is your sister? Isn't she the girl Jillian hired to help our mother?" Jackie asked. "Mom adores her. They're having a ball together."

"That's Clemmie! She loves Vivian, too. Our Grandmothers both live in Florida and we don't get to see either of them very often. For Clemmie, hanging out with Vivian is like having the world's coolest Grandmother living close by."

"I heard that they both came up to Northern Lights during a snow storm while Devlin was there in March," Dan said.

I blushed as I wondered just what details of that night Vivian had related to Devlin's parents.

Dan continued. "She said that you and Devlin stayed there in the storm without power to keep the generator going and the equipment running."

Jackie added, "And that you had a wonderful candlelit steak dinner in front of the fireplace. She always did like picnics. When Jilly and I were kids, she was always packing baskets and coolers full of food and drinks and taking us off somewhere for a picnic. I miss that." She turned to Dan. "When was the last time you and I took off somewhere and had a picnic? It's been forever. We need to be sure to do that sometime this summer."

Dan chuckled, "How about a sandwich together in the vineyard? Does that count as a picnic? Seems to be all we have time for in the summer, with all the work that needs to be done here."

"Jillian and Tommy got away for a whole week for their cruise. We should be able to manage at least an afternoon for a picnic."

David spoke up, "When was the last time you two had a vacation? Devlin and I can run things here. Dad, take her away somewhere."

"We could go to France or Italy," Jackie suggested.

"Or Niagara Falls," Dan said with a grin. "It's closer. Remember when we went there on our honeymoon?"

"I remember our honeymoon, but did we even see the Falls?"

David looked at me and said, "Here they go again. Want to help me clear the table? We'll leave these two lovebirds here." We cleared the table. David washed the dishes and I dried, while Jackie and Dan talked quietly at the table. By the time we were finished, they had decided.

"I'm calling a travel agent tomorrow morning," Jackie announced.

Dan added, "A trip to Napa Valley will give us a chance to visit the vineyards and wineries there. It'll be a working vacation – research."

Jackie hugged him. "It sounds wonderful! I can't wait. David, thank you for suggesting it. Chloe, do you like to shop as much as your sister? Maybe tomorrow we can hit the mall and see what we can find for me to wear in California."

We agreed to meet in the morning for our shopping excursion. I said good-night to the Carmichaels, who all gave me big hugs. I pulled on my fleece jacket and drove, very carefully, after all of that chianti, back to Devlin's house.

Jackie, Dan and David had made me feel so comfortable that I almost, but not quite, didn't miss Devlin.

* * *

Chapter 17

POISON IVY

Chloe

It was late when I got back to Devlin's house. I let myself in and headed upstairs to the bedroom. I stripped off my clothes, put Devlin's t-shirt back on, opened my cell phone and called him. He answered right away.

"How was dinner with my parents?" he asked. "I'll bet you had Mom's famous spaghetti."

"It was great, your family is great, and yes we had spaghetti and that was great, too. And I heard all about Woodstock. You never told me that they actually met there. That's so cool."

"Yeah? I've been hearing about Woodstock my entire life. I'm just glad they didn't name me Woodstock. Good thing they had the dog first."

I laughed and sighed, "I just wish you were here too. I had to work hard at restraining myself from kissing your brother again."

"Oh yeah? What about Dad?"

"Him, too," I replied. "You Carmichael men are so handsome!"

"Aww, you're making me blush." He changed the subject. "What are you doing right now?"

"I'm lying in your bed wearing nothing but one of your t-shirts and thinking about you," I answered in my best sexy voice.

"Oh Chloe, you're killing me. I'm in the guest room at Aunt Jilly's house all by myself, thinking about you. It's so lonely here without you. This is the last time I'll try to surprise you."

We talked for a long time and when we finally hung up, I was sleepy. I snuggled deeper under Devlin's comforter, hugged his pillow, and was asleep in seconds, dreaming of Devlin.

In my dream, he came quietly into the bedroom, undressed and slid into the bed next to me taking me into his arms. I reached for him and put my hands on his hard, muscled chest and felt – Boobs!?!

Instantly I was wide awake and screaming. There was a girl, a naked girl, in bed with me. And she was screaming too!

I scrambled over to the edge of the bed and knocked over the lamp when I tried to turn it on.

"Where's Devlin? Who are you? Where's Devlin?" the other girl was yelling. I finally managed to get a light turned on.

She was young, and beautiful, with long brown hair curling softly to her shoulders, and she was very naked. Those boobs I'd just been fondling were at least a C cup, very perky, and tipped with rosy pink nipples. Who was she? If Devlin had a girlfriend who was used to showing up naked in his bed in the middle of the night, I thought he might have mentioned it. I grabbed my cell phone.

"Don't call the police!" she yelled. "Just tell me where he is."

"Who are you? And what are you doing here?" I asked, my hand on the keyboard ready to dial. I wasn't about to tell her I was alone here until I got some answers.

At least she had stopped screaming. "And put your clothes back on." The sight of a strange naked girl in Devlin's bed was too much.

She glared at me. "I'm Ivy. Please don't call the police."

"I'm calling Devlin," I told her as I pressed redial.

"You've got his number?" she gasped, impressed.

Devlin answered on the fourth ring. "Umm, you missing me again?" he asked sleepily.

"Devlin, there's a girl here named Ivy who climbed into your bed naked. Do you know her?"

"Oh God, Chloe, I'm so sorry!"

My heart sank. It did, literally. That's another one of those sayings that I never believed. But I could feel my heart sinking in my chest. My heart's been doing a lot of sinking and leaping today. Ivy must be his girlfriend and he had kept her a secret from me. He was still talking but I wasn't getting it until I heard the words "restraining order".

"What? Say that again."

"She's been stalking me for months. I got a restraining order. Call the police. How did she get in?"

Relief flooded my body. She was his stalker, not his girlfriend.

Ivy was listening eagerly. "Let me talk to him," she asked. "Please."

"No!" I shouted. "And put your clothes on, or I am calling the police."

"Chloe, I'm calling Dad. You shouldn't be there alone with her."

I turned away from the bed and the sight of Ivy. "It's your body she's after, not mine. I don't think she's dangerous." I glanced over at Ivy. She was still sitting naked on the bed, but now she was crying instead of screaming.

"I just want to be with him," she sobbed.

I picked her clothes up from the floor and threw them at her. "For the last time, get dressed or I am calling the police."

Ivy gathered up her clothes and ran to the bathroom, slamming the door behind her.

Devlin was still on the line, but I could hear him talking to someone else. "Ivy's in my house with Chloe. Please go over there and get her out. Okay, thanks Dad."

"Chloe," he said to me. "I just called Dad on Tommy's phone. He's coming right over. Ivy's kind of nuts. She's been a problem, but she's never broken in before. Where is she now?"

"She's in your bathroom, getting dressed I hope."

"Okay, go downstairs to the front door. Dad will be there in a couple of minutes. Stay on the phone with me. You're doing great. She must have scared you, breaking in like this."

"At first, I thought she was you until I touched her chest and found boobs instead of muscles. Then, I thought maybe she was your girlfriend and you hadn't told me about her. I was kind of relieved when you told me she was just a stalker."

"Chloe," Devlin said to me over the miles. "Don't you know that you're my girlfriend, my only girlfriend. I'm sorry we haven't had much time together, but Chloe, I'm in love with you."

His words took my breath away. Another cliché that I was learning was true. I tried to take a deep breath to tell him that I loved him too, but just then, I heard Dan running up the front steps and across the porch. I opened the door. David was right behind him.

The both hugged me and checked that I was okay, then ran upstairs to deal with Ivy. Devlin was still waiting for me on the phone. "Devlin, they're here now, and I'm in love with you too!"

Suddenly, I realized that all I was wearing was Devlin's t-shirt and his dad and brother were coming down the stairs with a half dressed and very tearful Ivy. I dashed into the living room, grabbed a throw blanket off the back of the sofa and wrapped it around me, still clutching the phone.

Dan had a firm grip on Ivy's arm. "I'm taking her home. I know her parents and will tell them what happened. You're very lucky we don't call the police, young lady," he said to Ivy. "But this is the last straw. One more incident and you are going to jail." He marched her out the door. David stayed behind.

"I'm staying here the rest of the night," he said. "I'll sleep on the sofa, but we're not leaving you alone."

Devlin could hear all this over the phone. "Let me talk to Davy," he asked me. I handed Davy the phone.

"Chloe's okay," I heard him tell Devlin. Suddenly, now that the crisis was over, my legs were shaking and I sat down on the floor. "You are okay, aren't you?" David asked me. I nodded.

"She's just a little shaky. I'll check all the windows and doors and stay here on the sofa tonight. Do you want Bill to come change the locks again tomorrow? Okay, I'll call him. And don't worry, we'll take care of your girl. She looks real cute in your t-shirt." He winked at me and I pulled the blanket a bit tighter around my chest.

David handed the phone back to me and went to check the windows and doors. "Do you think you'll be able to get back to sleep?" Devlin asked me. It was two AM and I was wide awake. "There's some brandy in the wine cabinet. Have a glass and try to relax. You're safe now. I just wish I were there. I'd probably kill Ivy for scaring you like that if I were there, but I'd give anything to be there to hold you right now."

"I'm okay," I told him. "She's just a bit nuts. I feel kind of sorry for her. After all, she's crazy over you and you took out a restraining order against her."

"Crazy is the right word for her, all right. It's all because of that damn book. But enough about her. Get some of that brandy and try to get some sleep. Call me in the morning, sweetie."

"You get some sleep too. Don't worry about anything here. I'm okay. Good night, Devlin. I'm crazy about you too!"

I ran upstairs and put on some of Devlin's sweatpants and a Wild River sweatshirt that I found in his closet. In the kitchen, I found the brandy and poured two glasses, one for me and one for David. I took them into the living room where he was spreading a comforter out on the sofa.

"Medicinal brandy," I said, handing him a glass. "Dr. Devlin's orders. Thank you for coming to my rescue."

David grinned and bowed, "Anytime, m'lady. I live to rescue beautiful damsels in distress. Firebreathing dragons are my specialty but unfortunately, we have very few firebreathing dragons in upstate New York. I have to keep in shape by keeping Dev's groupies out of his house. Not a bad job when they are young, cute and nearly naked." He wiggled his eyebrows.

"My hero!" I told him, laughing at his goofiness.

I finished my brandy and yawned. "Let's get some sleep," I said to David. "I'll see you in the morning." He had finished his brandy and his eyelids were drooping.

"Try not to snore too loudly," he called after me as I headed back up the stairs.

I fell back into the bed and slept soundly until the bright morning sunlight streaming through the windows woke me.

* * *

Chapter 18

FAN CLUB

Chloe

"Oh, my God! She was in bed with you and you touched her boobs!" Mandy was doubled over with laughter.

It was the Thursday girl's night party after my *Meet the Parents* weekend. Mandy, Lil, Summer, and Skye were all howling with laughter, aided by several bottles of wine, at my story of finding Ivy in Devlin's bed with me.

"It's not that funny. She broke in to the house in the middle of the night. She might have been dangerous! Devlin and David call her Poison Ivy. She's been sending Devlin crazy messages and following him around for months. And, she stole my toothbrush!"

That set them off again. "What in the world did she want with your used toothbrush?" Skye asked, puzzled.

"I bet she thought it was Devlin's," Lil said. "And she wanted to do something kinky with it, like brush her pubic hair."

"Ewwwwww!" the rest of us all said. "That's disgusting!" Mandy added.

Summer piped in, "Was it an electric toothbrush? Maybe she wanted it to use as a vibrator."

"Ewwwwww!" we all said again.

"David has been watching for it to go up on Craig's List. He thinks she might try to sell it," I explained.

"How much is Devlin Carmichael's used toothbrush going for these days? Did you bring home any of his used boxer shorts or the hair from his shower drain?" Lil asked, still laughing. "You could have a profitable little side business going here."

"I don't think so," I answered, trying my best to be serious. "Devlin is really embarrassed by all of the attention he gets because of that book." The girls had all read the book and understood. "I sure don't want to contribute to that for a few bucks by selling stuff on Craig's List. He means too much to me to do that."

"Ohhh, that's so sweet!" Mandy hugged me. "You must really be crazy over this guy."

"Poison Ivy, Crazy Chloe. Sexy romance writer Devlin Carmichael's top fans! Can I join the club?" Skye asked with a giggle. "I'm the one who turned you on to the book."

"Chloe was turned on by Devlin, or should I say Joe, before she even got her hands on that book," Lil said. "I think her days of blind dating have finally come to an end. Right, Chloe?"

"I don't even look at other guys any more. I only want Devlin. I just wish he weren't so far away. I don't know how to do a long distance romance. At least we had 30 minutes in Detroit."

On Sunday, when I flew back to Traverse City and Devlin flew back to New York, we both had layovers in Detroit and managed to find each other for a whole half hour before we had to board different planes.

As soon as my plane from New York had landed, I was on my feet and out the door as fast as I could. I checked the arrival and departures board for Devlin's flight and groaned when I realized that his flight from Traverse City was landing on a different concourse about half a mile away. I slung my bag over my shoulder and took off as fast as I could in the crowds of people. I was afraid that I would pass him coming the other way and we would miss each other. There wasn't much time before my next flight took off.

I needn't have worried. We found each other. I felt myself pulled to him like he was a magnet and ran right into his arms.

"Chloe, Chloe," Devlin whispered as he kissed me. We stood in the middle of the concourse oblivious to the swarms of people swirling around us, until somebody told us to "get a room".

We broke apart, laughing. "If only we could," Devlin said softly. "We've only got a few minutes. Come on, I'll walk you to your gate. Are you okay? I'm so sorry about Ivy scaring you like that."

"It's okay," I teased him. "That's the price of having a boyfriend who's a celebrity. I guess I can deal with a few groupies. Maybe it's good that you weren't there to see her naked. She really does have great boobs."

"So do you, sweetie, and yours are the only ones I'm interested in seeing." We kissed again, blocking traffic and not caring.

"With Mom and Dad going to California next month, I probably won't be able to get away again for awhile," Devlin told me. I had called him the night before and shared the news. "I don't know when I'll be able to see you again."

"Do you think you can wait 'til June?" I asked him. "Can you come back then and be my date for Lil's wedding?"

"I wouldn't miss it for the world," he said and kissed me again.

"And Devlin…."

"Yes…."

"Bring David with you."

He looked at me. "What? One Carmichael man at a time is not enough for you?"

"Not for me! I want to introduce him to Clemmie."

* * *

Chapter 19

LILIANA'S WEDDING

Chloe

The month of May seemed to speed by in a whirl of preparations for Liliana's wedding. Wenonah held a bridal shower for Lil at Nokomis in early May. Evan came up to Traverse City for a couple of weekends for job interviews and house hunting. Then Lil went to East Lansing for his graduation. Luckily for me, Evan, the new Dr. McQuick, landed a job with a vet here in town and they would be staying in Traverse City. They found a nice house to rent between Nokomis and Evan's new job at the veterinary clinic and Lil and I spent every free minute getting it ready and moving in her things. I bought a new bed for her old room, now my guest room, and taped up paint swatches there and in the kitchen, looking for new colors for the white walls. Lil helped me shop for new cookware and utensils to replace her things that she was taking with her.

"You're going to have to give me cooking lessons, too," I told her. "I'm going to starve without you here, unless I pick up take-out from Nokomis every night and get lunch from Old Mission Deli."

"What about breakfast?" she asked, laughing. "Can you manage the coffee maker by yourself?"

"Coffee I can manage and I know where you live, remember. I'll be over for my muffin, scone, and cinnamon roll fix every time you bake." I hugged her. "I'm so happy for you but I'm going to miss you so much."

Devlin and I talked on the phone every day, counting down the days till we would see each other again.

Memorial Day weekend, the northern Michigan unofficial start of summer, was warm and sunny. The beaches were full of people even thought the water was still too cold for swimming. Sailboats flitted back and forth across Grand Traverse Bay, catching the breezes. The downtown shops and restaurants were filled with people. Northern Lights was busy too. The customers poured in the doors as fast as I could pour tasting samples for them. Sales were as good as the weather.

A week later, the wedding day was here.

No June bride on Old Mission Peninsula ever looked as beautiful as Liliana Oberlin. Her ivory silk dress was simple and perfect. She had let her short, spiky dark hair grow out a bit and Summer had styled it softly around her face, emphasizing her large, chocolate brown eyes and perfect cheekbones. Her grandmother's pearl necklace and new pearl earrings made by Mandy were her only accessories.

The wedding and reception were taking place at Northern Lights. The ceremony was to be outdoors near the vineyard overlooking Grand Traverse Bay. For the reception, a large white tent was set up adjacent to the tasting room. Tommy and Jillian had closed the winery to the public for the day. Only friends and family of the bride and groom would be there.

Lil, of course, had supervised the menu and all of the food was catered by Nokomis, Daughter of the Moon. Wenonah was overseeing the last-minute details helped by her staff from Nokomis who were guests today. Lil had hired students from the culinary college to help with the food and work as servers and bartenders at the reception.

For the Maid of Honor - me - actually the only bridesmaid, Lil and I had chosen a simple silk dress in a pale pink, the color of the silk cherry blossoms that Lil and I would carry in our bouquets. More silk blossoms, ivy, and grapevine decorated the tent and the dining tables.

Everything was beautiful – even the weather. It was a picture perfect Northern Michigan spring day. The temperature was in the low 70's, and the sky was as blue as the Bay, with just a few whipped cream-like clouds drifting serenely overhead.

My parents and Clementine were driving up from Bay City for the wedding, and since Lil had moved out, they planned to stay in my condo with me. How could I tell my parents that I wanted them to go to a hotel so I could finally have a night alone with Devlin? They haven't even met him yet. Clemmie has met him. That's why I asked him to bring David with him. I was hoping that Clemmie would be thrilled to meet a younger version of the guy she tried to call dibs on in March.

Lil and Evan's parents were all staying at the Bayshore Resort and I suggested to Mom that they might like to be there also. They've all been friends since we were kids, but she said that she could see them in Bay City anytime and she doesn't have as much time with me, her eldest daughter, as she would like. How could I tell her that I would rather be with Devlin then spend time with her and Dad. How can I tell Devlin that after waiting all this time, we still won't be alone together? It would be just too weird to have him there with Mom and Dad sleeping in the next room and Clemmie on the sofa in the living room.

I envied Lil and Evan their honeymoon suite at the Park Place Hotel. Would it be too tacky if Devlin and I slipped away from the reception for a few hours to use it? Oh, my God! I can't believe I even thought of something like that! Tacky, tacky, tacky! Maybe we'll just sneak over to Tommy and Jillian's house. It's closer. No, no, no! I can't do that either. I want the first time Devlin and I make love to be special, not a quickie in a borrowed bedroom.

Jillian had invited Lil and me to use her room to change into our dresses. Summer was there to help with hair and makeup. We all shared a bottle of Chloe Sparkles while we got ready. Lil was calm and cool as the proverbial cucumber. I was the nervous one, always checking out the window to watch for Devlin. He and David were driving this time. They had left very early this morning and should be here soon.

Jillian knocked on the door and came into the room. "Liliana, you are the most beautiful bride we have ever had here! And Chloe, you are sparkling even more brightly than usual."

Jillian was wearing a dress that Clemmie had found for her to wear on the cruise. It was a rich ruby red, a wrap style with a flowing skirt and a deep V neckline. The dress was perfect for her. Her hair was swept up off her neck into a loose chignon and she wore long dangling ruby red earrings with a matching necklace that Mandy had made for her. She looked gorgeous.

"Wow! Has Tommy seen you in that dress yet?" I asked.

She laughed. "We almost didn't make it to dinner the first night I wore it. From now on, I'm not buying any clothes without Clemmie's help. She really has a talent for fashion."

I heard the crunch of tires on the gravel drive below us and looked out the window. "Lil, your parents are here."

"Would you like me to go get them and bring them up here?" Summer asked. Lil nodded. "Don't cry. You'll smudge your mascara!"

Maria and Mike Oberlin were almost like second parents to me. Our mothers had met in the doctor's waiting room when they were both pregnant. Lil and I had been friends as long as we could remember. She was two weeks older than me and we had celebrated every birthday of our lives together, and much more besides. We'd been living together since college. She was closer to me than my sister, and I was going to miss having her around all of the time. I was thrilled that she and Evan would still be living in Traverse City.

Maria stepped quietly into the room and stood looking at Liliana with tears in her eyes. Lil hugged her. "Don't cry, Mama, or I'll start crying then Chloe will start crying and Summer will have to redo all of our makeup."

"Tears of joy for you," Maria smiled at her, wiping at her eyes. "You are so beautiful and I'm so happy for you and Evan. Your father wanted to wait and see you as you walk down the aisle with him. Is there an aisle? I've never been to a wedding in a vineyard before."

There was an aisle and Mike Oberlin proudly walked his daughter over the white runner spread through the grape vines to the alter set up in front of the white chairs filled with wedding guests. A group of music students from Interlochen Arts Academy was playing Aaron Copeland's *Appalachian Spring*. Evan, the handsome vet who had been Lil's boyfriend for many years, was waiting for her.

I had walked down that same aisle with Evan's best friend and Best Man. Mark and I knew each other well and had double dated with Lil and Evan a few times years ago. Nothing came of it but friendship. You can never have too many friends. Devlin and David were not here yet.

My parents and Clemmie were here. I've mentioned my parents a few times, maybe it's time I tell you a bit more about them. Barbara Clemmens and Kenneth Applewhite were high school sweethearts. He was a football player and she was a cheerleader. Barbie and Ken. After college, they got married and settled in Bay City where she is a physical therapist and he is a high school science teacher and football coach. They had two daughters, Clemmie and me.

I think Dad secretly wanted a son, but he's been a wonderful father, not minding that we preferred pink tutus and ballet slippers to football jerseys and cleats. Many of the boys on his teams became like surrogate sons and have kept in close touch with him over the years. I've even dated a few of them. I know Dad would love to have a son-in-law, but to his credit, he's never been critical of my serial dating and never encouraged me to settle down and get married.

Mom wants grandchildren, but she's in no hurry, thankfully. Maybe because Clemmie is so much younger than me and just graduated from high school, she, unlike many of my friends' mothers, was willing to wait. She had a miscarriage between Clemmie and me. They don't talk about it, but I think it was a boy. The son they never had. The brother I never had. I think about him sometimes and wonder what he would have been like and what it would have been like to have a brother.

Listening to Lil and Evan make their vows, I was overcome with emotion. Their wedding would mark a new chapter in our lives. They were now a grown up married couple. It seemed like yesterday that we were all just kids, and now they were planning on having kids of their own soon. Did I want that? Was I ready for that? Was Devlin the man I wanted to be with forever? Where was he?

"I now pronounce you man and wife. You may kiss the bride!" the minister said. They kissed. A tear rolled down my cheek.

Evan took Lil's hand in his and they walked together back down the aisle in the spring sunshine. I turned to follow, taking Mark's arm and there at the end of the aisle, waiting for me, was Devlin.

He smiled and I wanted to run past the bride and groom and throw myself at him, but Mark held my arm firmly and I had no choice but to keep pace with him. My eyes never left Devlin's all the way down the aisle. He looked great in gray dress slacks, white shirt, red tie, and a navy blue sport coat. I'd never seen him dressed up before and he looked more handsome than ever. Standing next to him was David, looking just as good. Oh, Clemmie was going to go nuts over David!

"I'm sorry," Devlin whispered when I was finally able to reach him. "We got held up in customs crossing over from Canada. It took hours."

"It doesn't matter. You're here now." I hugged him and I was so happy I could have cried, again.

Mom and Dad and Clemmie were walking up to us. Clemmie's eyes were wide with amazement. David's eyes were on Clemmie. She looked gorgeous in a sapphire blue dress, her long blond hair cascading over her shoulders like ripples of liquid gold. They didn't wait for introductions. David held out his hand to her and said "Hi." Clemmie said "Hello," took his hand, and they walked off together.

"Mom and Dad, I want you to meet Devlin." They all shook hands and Devlin added, "That was my brother, David, who just walked off with Clemmie. I think she's bewitched him. His manners are usually better than that."

Dad laughed, noting the way Devlin had kept his arm around me. "That's okay. Our girls often have that effect on men."

"I'm so happy to meet you, Devlin," Mom said, smiling at him. "Clemmie has told me a lot about you, including the fact that you are an author. Have you written anything I might have read?"

Oh, God! I hope not!

Devlin covered nicely. "Just one little story when I was in college, Mrs. Applewhite. It's probably not something you would like."

"Please, call me Barb,"

"And I'm Ken," Dad added.

"Let's go get a drink," I said and steered them towards the tent.

"Hey, Chloe! Looking good!" The bartender gave me a glass of wine and a big smile, ignoring Devlin.

"Matt! I didn't know you were going to be here today." I smiled back and handed the glass to Devlin. "I'd like you to meet my boyfriend, Devlin."

"Boyfriend, huh? You finally settling down?" Matt asked.

"You never know," I replied, accepting another glass of wine from him. "Thanks, Matt. See you later."

"Old boyfriend?" Devlin asked

"No, we just went out a few times."

"Chloe!" a voice shouted behind me. I turned and was immediately grabbed in a big bear hug. "It's been years! Remember me?"

He loosened his grip and I looked up. "Will!" I squealed. "You look great!" And he did. Lil's cousin, Will, was very tall and very handsome. "What are you doing now?"

"I'm developing a new resort in Aruba. You should come down and see it. Ever been to Aruba?" I shook my head and he continued. "It's a beautiful island with the perfect climate. I'd love to show it to you."

"Devlin," I said, grabbing his free hand. "This is Lil's cousin, Will. Will, this is my boyfriend, Devlin Carmichael. Maybe we'll come to Aruba together."

Will shook Devlin's hand and slipped me a business card. "Call me when you do. I'll give you the island tour and take you where the tourists don't go."

"Another old boyfriend?" Devlin whispered to me when Will left.

"Lil set us up on a blind date and we went out a few times, but he was in school in Ann Arbor, and too far away."

Devlin looked serious. "Ann Arbor is closer than New York. Am I too far away?"

"You're here now," I said softly, looking into his eyes. "We'll figure out the rest as we go because I love you and I will not let a few hundred miles come between us."

Devlin touched my cheek softly and gave me a gentle kiss. "I love you, too," he whispered in my ear.

"Hey, you two, is a wedding any place for public displays of affection?" Ben was suddenly standing beside Devlin, watching us with a grin.

"Hi, Ben. Meet Devlin."

Ben was eyeing Devlin carefully. "You'd better take good care of our girl here. She deserves only the best."

"Have you dated every guy at this reception?" Devlin asked me.

"Not every guy, she missed me." Dane stepped up to join us and put his arm around Ben. "But I adore her anyway."

I gave him a hug. "I adore you, too, Dane. He helped me decorate my condo," I explained to Devlin.

Dinner was about to be served and we found our way to our seats. Lil had seated Devlin next to me, and Mark's girlfriend, Carolyn, next to him, at the head table.

As always from Nokomis, the food was fabulous. We had salads of fresh spring greens, grilled asparagus, roasted leg of lamb, tender steak kabobs, tiny new potatoes and baby carrots in a creamy sauce. The service was perfect, and the Northern Lights wine was wonderful. We toasted the bride and groom with glasses of bubbling Chloe Sparkles.

After dinner, a local band played a great variety of oldies, classics, and new music. I danced almost every dance with Devlin. I left him long enough to dance once with my Dad and once with Evan. Clemmie and I changed partners halfway through one song so she could dance with Devlin and I could dance with David. I overheard her say to him, "Thank you for bringing David with you." I think she has transferred her crush from Devlin to David, just as I had hoped.

"Did you date anyone in the band?" Devlin asked me later as we slow-danced to *Stairway to Heaven*.

"Just Ringo," I replied.

"Ringo?"

I gave a little wave to the drummer and he winked at me in return, twirling his drumsticks with a flourish.

"Richard Starr is his real name. When he took up the drums, everybody started calling him Ringo and it stuck. We went out a few times. Mostly I just sat in the clubs and watched him play, but I'm not a groupie type girl and it got old in a hurry. He's a really nice guy. But not a nice as you," I added quickly, giving him a squeeze.

The song ended but Devlin didn't let go of me. We kept swaying to music only we could hear.

* * *

Jillian

We've had a lot of weddings here at Northern Lights over the years, but this was definitely my favorite. Liliana kept everything simple but elegant. I was serving as hostess, but also as a guest and having a great time. Tommy and I danced to our favorite old songs and I felt beautiful in my red dress. Best of all, my two handsome nephews were here.

I was watching Devlin and Chloe on the dance floor when Barb came and sat next to me. "Another wedding soon, do you think?" she asked me. "My daughter and your nephew. Will that make us related?"

I laughed. "I think so, I hope so. I always wanted a little girl and I've come to love Chloe like a daughter. I'd settle for being her aunt-in-law."

"And I'll happily take Devlin as a son-in-law. Maybe David, too," Barb added as Clemmie and David rushed by us, hand-in-hand, out of the tent and into the vineyard.

As we watched, Mandy and Ted's small son, Connor, ran across the dance floor and grabbed Chloe around her legs. "Aunt, Koee, dance with me," he demanded. Devlin reached down, lifted him up and held the toddler so he had one arm around each of them as they continued dancing. We could hear Connor's happy laughter ringing out over the sound of the band.

"How do you feel about grandchildren?" I asked Barb. Watching her watch the trio, I knew her answer already. "They'll make great parents."

"Maybe we should have gone to a hotel," Barb sighed. "We just assumed we'd stay at Chloe's place since Lil would be gone and she had an extra room. She won't tell me so, but I can see she'd rather have Devlin there, alone."

Here was my chance to play matchmaker, or fairy godmother, for Chloe. "If Devlin is going to stay at Chloe's place, we have room here. Why don't you stay here? I have two extra bedrooms. Davy can sleep on the sofa in the office. Tommy and I would love to have you, and I'll bet Clemmie would rather stay here, closer to Davy."

Barb considered my suggestion. "That's very nice of you, Jillian. I'm sure that would make Chloe and Devlin happy. They haven't been able to spend much time together. But let me talk to Ken. He still thinks of Chloe as his little girl, not a grown woman, especially not a grown woman with a sex life."

Chloe, you can thank me later - maybe even name your first child after me.

* * *

Blue Moon - A Dry Reisling this perfect only comes along once in a Blue Moon. Fabulous floral aromas, light and crisp, not sweet, with the flavors of apple, peach, and honey. The taste of the north in a blue bottle.

Chapter 20

I COULD HAVE DANCED ALL NIGHT

Chloe

When I was a little girl, I saw the movie *The King and I* on television and loved the song *Shall we Dance?* I thought the sight of Anna and the King of Siam waltzing across the palace floor was the most romantic thing ever.

My other favorite was Eliza in *My Fair Lady* singing and dancing to *I Could Have Danced All Night*. I knew just how Anna and Eliza felt. I was dancing on air.

That's how I felt at Liliana's wedding. I could have danced all night with Devlin. I'd kissed a lot of frogs, many of them were here tonight, but I'd finally found my prince. Unfortunately, like Cinderella at midnight, I'd be going home without him, or so I thought.

The band took a break and Devlin went to the bar to get us each a drink. Mom found me. "Having fun?" she asked with a grin. Oh-oh, something's up, I thought.

"Listen, honey, Jillian's invited your Dad, Clemmie, and me to stay here tonight. Would that be okay with you?"

Okay!?! I could hardly keep the happiness out of my voice. "Well sure, Mom, if you want. That's a great idea! You won't have to worry about drinking and driving back to my place. Oh, and in the morning, you should walk up to the ridge to see the sun come up over East Bay." Yeah, like any of us were going to be up before dawn tomorrow.

Devlin joined us holding three glasses of wine. He handed one to me and one to Mom. "To the lovely Applewhite ladies," he toasted.

Mom spoke right up. "Ken, Clemmie and I are going to stay here tonight so you and Chloe can have some privacy."

Devlin almost choked on his wine. I pounded him on the back and he coughed a couple of times to clear his throat. He didn't know what to say. I watched him try to keep his cool and be polite. He just met Mom a few hours ago and here she was practically telling him they would stay out of our way so we could sleep together tonight.

"Umm, Aunt Jilly's guest room is very nice. I'm sure you'll be very comfortable here. I always am."

Nice recovery, I thought and squeezed his hand. It was almost midnight and this Cinderella was ready to leave the ball – with her prince. But first, I had to find Lil and fulfill my Maid of Honor duties.

I found Lil after only a few minutes of looking. She was just saying good night to her parents who were leaving. Maria hugged me and said, "Are you next? We really like your young man."

"I like him too!" I answered, avoiding her question. Why is it that weddings always make matchmakers out of parents?

After Mike and Maria left, I took Lil aside. "Jillian has invited Mom, Dad, and Clemmie to stay here. Devlin is coming home with me!"

Lil smiled, "Finally, a night alone with your Prince Charming! Looks like we'll both have a good night tonight! Don't worry about anything here. Wenonah and Jillian will take care of anything that needs to be done. Just go and have a wonderful night!"

"Shouldn't I be saying that to you? It's your wedding night!"

"It's not like Evan and I have never slept together before. After all this today, we'll probably just collapse in bed and fall asleep as soon as we get to the hotel. Now go – and call me later with details!"

I gave her a final hug good-bye and turned to find Devlin. He was talking to Tommy and Dad and they looked serious. I joined them.

"Chloe, have you seen your sister?" Dad asked. "I've been looking for her for an hour and can't find her anywhere."

"David is missing, too," Tommy added.

"Then I'm sure they're together someplace," I told them. "They've been together through the whole reception."

"They can't have gone far," Devlin added. "My car is here. Davy didn't take it anywhere. They probably just went for a walk." Seeing the look of concern on Dad's face, he added, "Davy is very responsible. I'm sure she's okay. We'll find them."

Devlin quickly and efficiently put together a small search party. Mom and Jillian took the house, Dad and Tommy the tasting room and winery buildings and Devlin and I, armed with flashlights. headed out into the vineyard.

There was a full moon and we didn't need the flashlights. I kicked off my shoes and walked with Devlin through the rows of grape vines up to the ridge.

We heard them before we saw them, a soft voice and quiet giggle behind the vines. Devlin took my arm and motioned for me to keep quiet and circle around them to the left. He went right. We snuck up on them from opposite directions. We didn't really need to sneak. They were so engrossed in each other, a herd of elephants could have stomped through that vineyard without them noticing. Once we were in place, we flicked on the flashlights and Devlin yelled, "What are you kids doing out here?"

Clemmie shrieked and hid her head in David's chest. He wrapped his arms around her to protect her while yelling, "Who's that?"

Devlin started laughing and I spoke up, "Clementine Suzanne! Everybody's out looking for you. Dad's having a fit!"

Clemmie looked up but couldn't see me behind the beam of the flashlight. "Chloe? We just came out for walk to see the Bay in the moonlight. What's wrong with Dad?"

"He couldn't find you and got worried and got everybody all worked up to search for you. You'd better go back and let him know you're okay."

"It's my fault," David said. "I asked her to come out here with me."

"Then you'd better go apologize to her Dad if you ever want to be able to see her again," Devlin told him. "And brush the dirt off your pants before you do."

They stood up. Clemmie tried to brush the dirt off her dress. Her hair was a mess. I tried to comb it out with my fingers and pulled out a few leaves and bits of grape vine. "Doesn't Dad remember that I'm eighteen now?" Clemmie asked.

Devlin pulled his cell phone out of his pocket and called Tommy. "We found them up on the ridge. Yeah, they're fine, just wanted to see the Bay in the moonlight. Yeah, they are on their way back right now." He handed David his flashlight and we watched them walk back down the hill towards the tent.

We stayed up on the ridge for awhile, enjoying the night, the moonlight and the view. "This is nice," Devlin said, cuddling me closely. "We should have brought a bottle of wine."

"David and Clemmie did." I reached into the vines behind us and pulled out the blue bottle of Blue Moon Reisling that I'd seen Clemmie hide when we snuck up on them. "No glasses, we'll have to drink out of the bottle."

"Did they save any for us?"

I held the bottle up to the moonlight. "Not much. At least they have good taste in wine. When I was Clemmie's age, I was sneaking Boone's Farm."

We sat in the moonlight and smooched a bit, passing the bottle back and forth between us until it was empty. "Isn't it miraculous?" Devlin asked me.

"That we found each other?"

"Well, yeah, that too, but I was talking about this," and he took my hand and filled it with dirt from his hand. "This soil, this place. Here we are on the 45th parallel, halfway between the equator and the North Pole, on this peninsula, surrounded by Great Lake waters that temper the weather. All these factors in harmony to make the perfect climate to grow grapes."

I let the soil sift through my fingers back onto the ground.

Devlin continued, "From those grapes, people have been making wine for thousands of years, in thousands of varieties. That's what I want to do with my life, Chloe, continue that tradition, contribute to that history, and hopefully make people happy with the wines I make along the way. Are you okay with that? Before we take this relationship to the next level, I want you to know me. No mystery man, the real me. What I believe in, who I am. I'm not just Devlin Carmichael, the author of *Sweet Intoxications*. I'm Devlin Carmichael, grape farmer and winemaker."

I pulled a leaf from the vine and pressed it into Devlin's hand. "I chose this life, too. Well, maybe I kind of fell into it accidently when Jillian hired me, but I've come to love it - from the new growth of the vines in the spring, watching the grapes grow in the hot summers, the fall harvest, the pressing and fermentation, the bottling, and sharing our wine with the customers. For me to find a man who shares that passion is a miracle. I've been looking for you for a long time. I may like your book, but I'm not one of the *Sweet Intoxications* groupies. It's Devlin the grape farmer and winemaker that I am in love with."

"Well, great! Now that we have that clear, let's go to your place!" Devlin kissed me quickly, stood up, and offered me his hand to help me up. Devlin carried the empty blue bottle as, hand in hand, we walked back down the hill to the rest of our lives.

When we got back to the tent, it and the tasting room were deserted. The party was over. We took my car and Devlin drove slowly back to my condo. The last thing we wanted tonight was to hit a deer, or to be stopped for speeding, or drinking and driving, or going the wrong way on a one way street, or stealing a car.

We were silent as I led Devlin upstairs and inside. "Do you want something to drink?" I asked him, turning on the light inside the door.

He shook his head and reached me for me. "Chloe," he whispered softly in my ear, "Do you have a spare toothbrush? I forgot my bag. It's still in my car."

I laughed. Good thing we both stocked up on spare toothbrushes. I had needed one when Ivy stole mine at his house. I led him into my bedroom and turned on the lights. Devlin looked around in wonder. "This room is you! Who would ever think all these colors would look so good together?"

"I had lots of help. Dane is so talented. He understood what I wanted more than I did and pushed me to go a little wild. I love it!"

Devlin was studying the mermaid picture. "Yeah, I love it to."

I laughed and went into the adjoining bath to get him a new toothbrush. While he used the bathroom, I took off my shoes and my earrings, turned down the covers on the bed, and got a slinky nightie from my dresser. When Devlin came out, I kissed his toothpaste flavored mouth on my way into the bathroom. "Be right back," I told him.

I pulled off my dress and underwear, slid on the nightie, washed my face, brushed my teeth and hair, dabbed on a tiny bit of perfume, tuned off the light, and opened the door. Devlin was in my bed, his clothes in a pile on the floor. I slid in next to him and he welcomed me into his arms.

Being there together, in my bed with its French bordello headboard, on that night, felt so right and so comfortable that we both fell asleep. Okay, so I had been looking forward to this with so much anticipation but it was such an emotional day, with Lil getting married and everything, and Devlin had left very early and drove all the way from New York. We were both exhausted. I slept like a baby.

The sound of the rain woke me. From the dim light coming from my windows, I couldn't tell if it was still night or very early morning. Devlin was awake too. He had turned on his side to face me. "I'm sorry," he said softly. "How could I have fallen asleep?"

"It's okay, I did too. We both needed it."

He traced the line of my cheek softly with his finger and pushed my hair back from my face. "You're beautiful in the morning, Chloe Louise!"

"Thank you, Devlin Joseph. You look pretty good yourself, even with this morning stubble." I kissed him, rubbing his cheek. "You may have to grow a beard, or borrow a pink ladies razor this morning."

"Is it morning? Let's pretend it's still night. I want to make love to you." His hand trailed down from my cheek, to my neck, across my collarbone, to dip to the edge of my nightgown across the tops of my breasts. I shuddered with pleasure.

"Morning, noon, or night. Rain or shine. Now is good, very good." I wrapped my arms around him, ran my fingers through his sleep tousled hair and pulled him to me.

Devlin's mouth found mine. Our kisses were no longer gentle and tasting, but eager and biting.

I closed my eyes and tried to slow my breathing. I opened my eyes and saw his face in the dim light watching me. "Let me love you," Devlin whispered softly.

Here is where words fail me. How to describe that moment of perfect pleasure? The earth moved, our souls merged, fireworks exploded. All clichés, all true, but not true enough to describe what I felt with Devlin.

A sudden bolt of lightning lit the room, followed immediately by a loud clap of thunder. The rain pounded on the windows like it was trying to break into our room to escape the storm. It was almost as though the passion we created in the bedroom had spread to the skies and created the lightning and thunder.

Exhausted, we slept again.

* * *

Chapter 21

AFTERGLOW

Chloe

When I woke up again, morning sunshine was pouring in through the windows. The thunder storm had passed. I could smell coffee and hear sounds coming from the kitchen. Lil must be cooking breakfast. Then I remembered – Lil was gone, married to Evan and on her honeymoon. Devlin was here. I stretched and yawned. Happy as a dog with a bone. Happy as a cat in the cream. Happy as a bird with a French fry. Happy as a girl in love whose lover was serving her breakfast in bed.

Devlin came into the room with a smile…and a tray. He was wearing boxer shorts and the dress shirt he wore yesterday to the wedding, unbuttoned. He looked good, good enough to eat, but my stomach rumbled at the sight of the tray. I was hungry.

"Good morning!" Devlin greeted me, setting down the tray to give me a kiss. "I found stuff for breakfast. Sleep okay?"

"Best night of my life!" I told him, sitting up with the sheets barely covering my breasts.

"Me, too! What do you say we have breakfast and then see what we can do about making this the best day of our lives?"

We dug into the food - coffee and juice, fresh strawberries and muffins, laughing and feeding each other. Soon the food was forgotten as we became lost in each other again, and again, and again. The strawberry stains may never come out of the sheets. Do I care? Not one bit!

It was my ringing phone that brought us up for air. I reached out for it and glanced at the caller ID - Mom. I took a deep breath to try to compose myself before I answered.

"Hi Chloe, hope you had a good night?"

How was I supposed to answer that? Oh well, if she ever reads this account, she will know. "It was great, Mom. Thank you."

"That's nice, honey. I'm happy for you. Dad and I would like to get to know Devlin a little better. Could the two of you meet us for a late lunch before we head back today? I was thinking about two o'clock at North Peak?"

"Sure, Mom! That would be nice. We'll see you there." I clicked the phone shut and told Devlin about the plan. "What time is it now?"

He looked at my bedside clock, "One-fifteen! Guess we'd better get up. You do realize that the only clothes I have here are what I wore yesterday?"

"I forgot. I do have one of your Wild River t-shirts here, but it's in the laundry. I stole it from your house and sleep in it all the time. Why don't you call David and see if he can bring your bag over here. I'm going to get in the shower."

Devlin grinned at me. "You've been sleeping in my t-shirt? Maybe I should wear that today."

I picked up his phone from the pile of his clothes on the floor and tossed it to him. "No way! Call Davy."

A few minutes later, when I had my hair lathered with shampoo, Devlin stepped in behind me. "Need your back washed?" he asked with a smile.

This time it was the doorbell that interrupted us. "That's gotta be Davy with my bag." Devlin rinsed off, stepped out of the shower, grabbed a bath towel and wrapped it around his hips as he went to open the door.

It was David with his bag, and Clemmie. "Hi, Devlin," she grinned at him, "Need some clothes?" He grabbed the bag and dashed back to the bedroom.

"We'll just wait for you out here," David added.

I was out of the shower and into some clothes – a summer skirt and purple t-shirt - in record time. I quickly blew my hair dry while

Devlin found his razor and shaved. He found shorts and a polo shirt in his bag and slid his feet into a pair of boat shoes. I pulled on sandals and we were ready.

North Peak is a micro brewery and restaurant on the west end of Front Street in downtown Traverse City. The three story yellow brick building started life as a candy factory a hundred years ago. Now, it's Dad's favorite Traverse City eating spot. He loves the wood-fired pizzas and the handcrafted beer. The rest of us stuck with iced tea, lemonade, and cokes to drink.

Clemmie waited till he had his first beer and slice of pizza before asking, "Dad, school's out and I don't start my summer job 'til Friday. David and Devlin are staying a few days and David offered to take me back to Bay City when they leave. Can I stay here with Chloe, please, please, please?"

Dad looked from her to David, then to me and Devlin. I could just imagine what he was thinking. My face and neck were red, not from blushing this time but from the burn of Devlin's whiskers on my skin.

"You'll be staying at Chloe's place?" he asked. "And David will be staying…"

"With Aunt Jilly and Uncle Tommy," David added quickly. "Sir, on my honor, I promise you can trust me to take good care of Clementine. I will not let any harm come to her."

Dad looked at me, "Chloe? Is this okay with you?" he hesitated, "And Devlin?"

"Dad!" Clemmie interjected. "Remember, I'm eighteen now. That means I'm legally an adult."

"Yes, legally, but …"

"Dad, it's okay. It's just a couple of days and we'll be together all of the time. Please let her stay." I couldn't believe I was pleading to have Clemmie stay with me while Devlin was here, but there it was.

Mom spoke up, "Ken, she'll be away at school in a few months. You have to let go sometime. She'll be fine here with Chloe."

"We'll be going to Bay City to see our grandmother on Tuesday. We'll be happy to bring Clemmie back then," Devlin told him. I could see that Dad was impressed. Young men who visit their grandmothers were okay in his book, even if his daughters were involved with them.

I was thinking about Tuesday. That gave us only the rest of today and all day Monday together. Then Devlin was going back to New York – 600 miles away. How were we going to do this? Devlin couldn't leave his home and his family business to live here. Could I leave my job and my home to go there? Could we maintain a long distance relationship without being together physically? Not after last night and this morning. Clemmie wanted a couple of days. I wanted more.

Devlin was watching me as though he could read my mind. He squeezed my hand under the table and smiled at me. We would find a way to be together, he was telling me, and I believed him.

Clemmie changed the subject. "David told me that NYU has a great fashion program. Maybe I should look into going there in September."

"You've already been accepted at Ferris State. Have you looked into out-of-state tuition? Do you know what that would cost? The only way you're going to NYU is if you could get a full scholarship!"

Good move, Clemmie! Dad was focused on the cost of school now, not what his girls were doing with the Carmichael men.

"How's you pizza, Dad?"

"I love this cherry chicken salad. I've got to pick up a box of dried cherries before we leave Traverse City," Mom said. She was good at changing subjects also.

"I'll get them for you, Mom, and bring them home on Tuesday," Clemmie offered.

After lunch, Mom and Dad left. Clemmie stayed. "I get that you want to be alone with Dev," she told me. "Davy and I will just hang out, maybe go to a movie or something.

I was tempted, but eighteen or not, she was still my baby sister. "We'll all hang out – together. Let's show the guys the Sleeping Bear Dunes. It'll be fun."

So we spent the rest of the afternoon, the four of us, being tourists at the Sleeping Bear National Lakeshore. After the morning rain storm, the sky had cleared and the day turned beautiful. We drove west to the little town of Empire, then took the scenic drive over the top of the dunes. We stopped at the overlooks and ran like little kids down the ancient sand hills on the shore of Lake Michigan, laughing, chasing, and tumbling in the sand.

Sitting on the top of a giant sand dune, looking west over the great lake towards the Manitou Islands, David asked, "Why is it called Sleeping Bear? Are there bears here?"

"The name comes from an old Native American legend," I explained. "Long ago, on the far shore of the lake in Wisconsin, a mother bear and her two cubs swam into Lake Michigan to escape a forest fire. After swimming for many hours, the bear cubs got tired and lagged behind their mother. The mother bear reached the shore and climbed this bluff to watch and wait for her babies. But the cubs were not quite strong enough to make the long swim and they drowned right out there." I pointed to the islands. "The Great Spirit created the two islands to mark the spot where the cubs disappeared and the spirit of the mother bear lives in this dune, always watching and waiting for her babies."

Devlin took my hand. "That's a sad story for such a beautiful place."

After the Sand Dunes, we followed M-22 around the peninsula that forms Michigan's little finger through Leland, Northport, Sutton's Bay, and back to Traverse City. In Glen Arbor, we stopped at Cherry Republic so Clemmie could buy dried cherries for Mom. Devlin bought some for Vivian and Jackie and I picked up a box for Lil. Maybe she would make me more cherry scones. How was I going to eat with her no longer living in my condo and cooking for me every day?

We stopped at a few of the wineries along the way. Devlin and I tasted some Leelanaw County wines and he bought a few bottles to take home. We let David drive after that.

Why is it that we don't take time to be tourists in our own home towns? There is so much to see and do here, but I don't always take advantage of it as I should. Maybe I was seeing it through fresh eyes today. Maybe it was because I was thinking about going to New York to be with Devlin that I was now seeing my home with new appreciation.

It was late when we got back to my condo. We'd picked up Chinese food for dinner and we carried it out to the balcony. The sky was still clear and the moon was one night past full. I opened a bottle of Sugar and Spice Gewurztraminer for Devlin and me. Clemmie and David had Cokes. We sat outside on the balcony and ate the food and drank the wine and talked and laughed and had a really great evening. But I was ready for David to leave and Clemmie to go to bed so I could go to bed, too, with Devlin.

Devlin was yawning and shooting David meaningful looks, but David was ignoring him. He only had eyes for Clemmie and she was showing no signs of ending the evening.

Finally, as the clock was striking midnight, I spoke up. "Listen, I need to go into work in the morning for a bit. I have to get some sleep, so David, can you find your way back to Northern Lights okay?"

"You and I need to help Tommy with that new equipment in the morning," Devlin added.

"So I can sleep in while the rest of you work," Clemmie giggled.

David looked crestfallen. "You won't be coming with them? I wanted to show you the view from the ridge in the daylight."

She smiled sweetly at him, "Okay, I'll be there. Come on, Davy, these two lovebirds," she nodded towards me and Devlin, "want to go back to their nest."

We picked up the glasses, bottles, and empty food wrappers and headed back inside. "It's not fair," Clemmie said to me as we were putting the dishes in the dishwasher. "You get to have Devlin stay here with you, but David has to leave. Dad wouldn't have to know if he stayed." She batted her eyes and tried out her most winning smile, but it didn't work on me.

"Clemmie Sue! You just met him yesterday. I don't care if you are eighteen now, you are not sleeping with him in my house."

"God! You sound just like Dad," she snorted.

I laughed, "I do, don't I? Listen, little sister, I just want you not to rush into anything. I know it's hard to wait and David is just as irresistible as his big brother, but I care about you and don't want you to be hurt if it doesn't work out." I gave her a hug. "Now go say good-night. You'll see him again tomorrow."

Clemmie went to the door with David. Devlin and I headed into my room to give them privacy to say good-night.

I heard the front door close, then Clemmie went into Lil's room to get ready for bed. My room was separated from Lil's by my bathroom and walk-in closet but sounds still carried a little bit. We would have to be quiet tonight.

"This has been a wonderful day," Devlin whispered to me as I snuggled against him under the covers on the strawberry stained sheets. We didn't have time to wash them today. The night had turned cool and his body was warm next to mine. I hadn't bothered with a nightgown tonight. Last night's discarded nightie was still on the floor by the bed. One flimsy strap had somehow gotten torn. I might keep it as a reminder of our first night together.

On our second night together, we took our time and made love tenderly, slowly, quietly, and oh, so sweetly until, satisfied and exhausted, we fell asleep in each other's arms.

* * *

Chapter 22

FOUR PLAY

Jillian

It was two days after Liliana's beautiful wedding and romance was still in the air at Northern Lights. Chloe and Devlin were so obviously in love it made me happy just to look at them. Clementine and David were flush with the excitement of a new romance. Two brothers, dark and handsome. Two sisters, blond and beautiful. Amazingly right for each other. The old winery felt like a fairy tale setting that day with the four of them there. I said a little prayer for them all, for true love and happily ever after.

Tommy felt it too. I was working in the tasting room with Mandy when he called me out to the barrel room. "What do you need?" I asked hurrying out between customers. He jumped out from between two barrels, grabbed me and kissed me. "I need you, baby!" he murmured while nibbling my neck. "Wanna fool around behind the barrels?"

I laughed and kissed him back. "Ouuuuu, you make me so hot!" I was hot, but it came in flashes. I was coping better with the hot flashes since the cruise. I just closed my eyes, took slow breaths, and imagined that I was having my own personal tropical mini vacation. Worked like a charm.

"Hey, you two!" Oops, Davy had walked in on us. "Remember, you are supposed to be chaperoning the kids here. What kind of example are you setting for us?"

Us? I looked around the barrel. Clemmie was with him. She hadn't voluntarily left his side since they met on Saturday. Poor girl. I could imagine the heartbreak she would feel tomorrow when the boys left to go home. Clemmie and Chloe both.

Tommy answered for us, "The best kind of example. We've been married for 30 years and we're still madly in love. Take my advice, young Davy. When you find a woman like your Aunt Jilly, marry her, cherish her, take care of her, and she will make you happy forever."

"Ummm, a woman like my Aunt Jilly would be my Mom!"

"I didn't mean exactly like Jilly. I mean smart, and beautiful, and funny, and sexy..." he hesitated.

"And hot," I added playfully. "Don't forget hot!" I kissed him again, gave him a loving slap on the butt and, smiling, headed back into the tasting room. I'd collect on the fooling around later.

I really was incredibly lucky. Tommy and I were very happy together, still had a great sex life, no health problems, and had a good business that we both loved. We enjoyed working together. We enjoyed just being together. The only thing missing from our lives was children. We had wanted them, but it just hadn't happened. We'd had the tests and had undergone some procedures, but no luck. We'd talked about adoption, but hadn't gone through with it, always thinking that someday we would have our own.

I was thrilled to have my sister's sons here for a few days, and happy to see that Devlin and Chloe were so much in love. I hoped that meant that we would see much more of Devlin here, not that we would lose Chloe to Wild River.

* * *

Chloe

Devlin, David and Tommy had finished installing and testing the new equipment. Jillian made sandwiches for everybody and brought them out to the tasting room at noon. Devlin and I wrapped two sandwiches in napkins and took them, an old blanket, two wine glasses, and a bottle of Chloe Sparkles and headed out into the vineyard by ourselves. Sparkling wine is a good choice for a picnic – you don't have to take a corkscrew.

We climbed to the top of the ridge where we had the best view of Grand Traverse Bay, spread out our blanket, and sat in the spring sunshine. There is a store in town that sells t-shirts with the logo *Life is Good*. They are decorated with drawings of a stick figure guy and his dog doing simple, good things to enjoy life. I'll have to look for one with a boy and a girl having a picnic in a vineyard. Life was good, very good, today, here, on this hilltop, with Devlin. The only thing that kept it from being perfect was the thought that tomorrow he would be going back to New York.

"I've been thinking." Devlin took my hand. "How does this sound? David's out of school for the summer and helping at Wild River. If I work ten days in a row and take four days off, I can come here every two weeks to see you."

"That's a lot of travel for you," I started. Devlin looked concerned, like I was going to say I didn't want to see him that often. "How about if I work the same schedule and every other time, I come to you?"

"Sounds like a plan!" Devlin kissed me, popped the cork, and poured. We clinked glasses and drank. We had a plan - we would see each other every other week, for the summer anyway.

That night, in my bed, under the watchful gaze of the mermaid, with soft pink light glowing from the lamp we had left on, we made love again, quietly, aware of Clemmie sleeping in Lil's old room down the hallway. We were naked under the soft sheet, touching, exploring each other's bodies. Finding new ways to please each other, we made love until sated and exhausted, we fell asleep, our limbs so tangled that I couldn't be sure where my body ended and his began.

Three nights together and he had to leave early in the morning. It was still dark when the alarm went off. Devlin tried to slide out of bed quietly but I woke up and pulled him back to me. "One more for the road?" I whispered and he obliged.

When I finally let him out of bed and into the shower, I put on my robe and went to wake up Clemmie.

"David will be here soon. Better get up. Time to go home."

"I'm awake," she mumbled.

I went back to my room, dropped the robe and stepped into the shower with Devlin. He turned around to face me and I wrapped my arms around him, pressing my breasts into his chest as he slid his soapy hands around my butt. "Oh Chloe, you make it very hard for me to leave."

"Hmmm, what was that?" I murmured lifting my head. "I'm making something hard?" And I reached down to check as Devlin's mouth found mine under the spray of hot water.

The doorbell rang. "Let Clemmie get it," he moaned. "It must be David."

The doorbell rang again. "She probably fell back asleep. I'll go." I slid, slippery with soap, out of Devlin's grasp, slipped into my robe, and went out through the dark living room to the door.

David looked at me, dripping and clad only in my robe. "Good morning! Everybody up and ready?" He was much too cheerful.

"Devlin's in the shower and Clemmie must still be in bed. You go try to wake her up, please." I steered him to Clemmie's door and he went in with a grin. How much trouble could they get into at six AM? I didn't want to spend my last minutes with Devlin trying to get Clemmie out of bed.

When I got back to my room, Devlin was out of the shower and pulling on shorts and a Wild River t-shirt. He had almost finished packing his clothes and toiletries. "Keep this toothbrush here for me," he asked, pressing it into my hand. "I'll be back soon."

"I'm going to miss you," I told him sadly.

He stopped what he was doing and slid his hands into my robe, circling my waist and pulling me to him. "In only ten days, you'll be in New York. I'll show you the lakes and take you kayaking down the river. I'll take you to my favorite restaurants and introduce you to my friends. Maybe we'll even have time to fool around a bit. How does that sound?"

"It sounds like Heaven, especially the last part. I'll be counting down the days." One last hug and kiss and I stepped away to let him finish his packing. Devlin glanced down at his t-shirt. I laughed. "I've left my mark on you!" Two wet round impressions marked the front of his shirt.

"You need some help drying off?" He asked with a lecherous grin.

"Sure!" I dropped my robe.

Twenty minutes later, Devlin got dressed again, I pulled on some sweats, and we suddenly remembered David and Clemmie.

"It's awfully quiet out there. We'd better go check on them." Clemmie's door was still open. We peeked in. Instead of waking her up, David had climbed into bed with her, fully dressed. He was spooned up against her back. Both of them were sound asleep.

With a glance and a nod, Devlin and I were in agreement. I got in next to David and he got in next to Clemmie. Tight squeeze, four of us in a queen size bed. "Wake up, sleepyheads!" I called out to them. "Who wants breakfast?" Devlin added.

David woke first. "What…?" In the light from the hallway, he saw Devlin's smiling face over Clemmie's shoulder. He jumped and guiltily backed away from Clemmie, pushing me off the other side of the bed as he did.

"Ow," I yelled as I hit the floor. Clemmie finally woke up. "What's going on?" she asked rubbing her eyes and finding herself in bed between David and Devlin, she smiled. "I must be dreaming," and she went back to sleep.

"Clementine Suzanne Applewhite! Wake up now!"

Her blue eyes opened again and she stretched like a cat. "You don't have to yell."

The guys went to the kitchen to make coffee and I stayed until I was sure Clemmie was awake and headed into the bathroom. It had been fun having her and David, and of course Devlin, here. Now they were leaving, Lil was gone, living with Evan, and I would be living alone for the first time in my life. I'd thought about getting another roommate, but the only roommate I wanted now was Devlin.

I could only hope that the next ten days would go by as quickly as the last three. We'd discussed our schedule with Jillian. She was good with it, very happy that we wanted to work out a way to be together. Devlin had booked a plane ticket for me. I was going back to Wild River, and this time Devlin would be there too, waiting for me.

Clemmie came out of the bathroom, awake, fresh, and happy to have a few more hours to spend with David. "We're all going to see Vivian. Then the guys will drop me off at home before they head to New York."

"Don't forget the dried cherries for Mom." I handed her the bag from Cherry Republic. "Have you got everything?"

She checked the room and found a pair of her shoes under the bed. She added them to her bag and zipped it up. "I guess I do. Thanks for letting me stay."

I hugged her. "Anytime, sis. I don't get to see you enough."

The coffee was ready and the guys had found cereal, bananas and the last of the muffins that Lil had left for me. Clemmie ate a banana and I nibbled on a muffin. We were all quiet.

David finished his bowl of cereal. He and Clemmie carried her bag and Devlin's out to the car, giving us a last moment alone.

"I'll be at the airport to pick you up in ten days," Devlin told me.

"I'll call you every day. I love you." I kissed him one last time and he was gone. I went back to bed, alone.

* * *

WILD RIVER WINERY

Chloe

By the calendar, September is still summer. Often, in Michigan, like upstate New York, September days are warm as summer, good for boating, hiking and swimming. But the days are shorter and the evenings cooler. The nights are perfect for lovers.

This was my third trip to Wild River since Devlin and I had started our plan. I kept very busy between visits with working, never taking a day off when we were apart. In July, Devlin had come to Michigan and we celebrated my 29th birthday with my parents and Clemmie. We had the usual cake with sparklers instead of candles then watched the fireworks over Grand Traverse Bay.

Clemmie and David became e-mail and Facebook friends. A week after David went back to New York, Clemmie met a new guy who was going to attend Ferris State in September also. She dropped her plan of applying to NYU. I won't be surprised when she finds another guy every week after she hits campus.

Now it was September and David, who had also found a new girlfriend, was back in school. Harvest was starting, and Devlin was going to be too busy to come to Traverse City this month and maybe not even next month. Even now, he was needed at the winery and we could only squeeze in a few hours of free time while I was here.

That was okay with me. While Devlin was working, I was at the winery also. I was learning the other side of the business from him, the blending, fermenting, and bottling processes. When I could, I also helped Jackie out in the office or the tasting room. I felt very much at home there with her, almost like working with Jillian at Northern Lights. I felt very much at home in Devlin's house also. I kept extra clothes and toiletries there so when I flew back and forth, I didn't have to bring anything. Our plan had worked well for the summer, but the cost of plane tickets took a big bite out of my savings and with no roommate sharing expenses, I was starting to worry about how long we could keep going back and forth between Michigan and New York.

This afternoon, Devlin was taking a break from work and had promised me a special treat, a surprise, and he was not giving any hints. It was a beautiful late summer day, clear blue sky, warm sunshine, and a slight breeze that teased us with just the tiniest hint of autumn. The mums were in bloom and the maples were showing their fall colors. A college football game was playing on the radio.

"Be ready at four o'clock," he had told me.

"Ready for what? What should I wear?"

He looked me over. I was wearing jeans, a Wild River polo shirt, and tennis shoes. "You're perfect just the way you are, but bring a sweatshirt or fleece jacket. It might get cooler where we're going."

I thought I'd gotten over my mystery date thing, but maybe not completely. I was excited. Of course this time I knew who I was going to be with, just not where we were going or what we were going to be doing. Devlin had disappeared a couple of hours ago while I'd been in the tasting room with Jackie. It had been a busy afternoon and she was glad to have the extra help. I couldn't help but wonder what he was up to as I watched for him to come back.

At 3:55, there was still no sign of him. I went into the ladies room to get ready. Hair combed, lipstick applied, carrying my fleece jacket and a hat, I walked outside to look for him. Jackie came out also, carrying a camera.

Just then, I heard what sounded like the clip-clop of horse hooves coming down the lane. There was Devlin, riding a big white horse, coming to get me, just like in my favorite fairy tales.

"My hero!" I shouted. "Where did you get him? He's beautiful!"

"Remember way back on our first date, I told you that I knew where to borrow a white horse. This is Snowball. Snowball, meet Princess Sparkles." He gave me a carrot and showed me how to feed it to Snowball. His lips were soft and his breath was warm as he gently took the carrot from the palm of my hand - Snowball's lips I mean, not Devlin's.

Devlin's lips were soft and warm too as he kissed me there in the parking lot by the white horse with his mother taking pictures and Wild River customers applauding.

"Come, m'lady, mount your noble steed and ride with me into the sunset." Devlin boosted me up on Snowball's back and got on behind me.

I laughed, and so did several of the customers. Mounting my noble steed sounded very sexy. What's that country song – *Save a Horse, Ride a Cowboy?* I was ready to ride both.

Devlin's arm tightened around me and I snuggled into his chest. He picked up the reins, clicked a signal to Snowball, shouted "Hi-ho, Silver," and we rode away.

"Oh, Devlin! What a perfect surprise! Thank you so much, I love this, and I love you!"

"Princess, this is only the beginning of your surprise. The best is yet to come." We rode down the long drive, out to the road, past Devlin's house, and turned into a path in the woods beyond.

The path wound through the trees, sometimes following a noisy little creek, up the hills for several miles. We finally emerged into a small natural clearing in the woods. Late summer wildflowers bloomed in the tall grass. The creek sparkled in the sun as it flowed in a twisting path through the clearing and back into the woods. In the center of the clearing stood one magnificent old maple tree, its leaves blazing deep scarlet against the blue sky. It took my breath away.

"Devlin, what is this place? It's magical!"

He reined Snowball to a stop. "I'm glad you like it. I found it when I was a little boy and it's always been my special secret place. I don't think anyone else knows about it or comes here. It's on our land, but we've never cleared or planted out here, just left it natural. It's really not far from Wild River. We took the long way here."

"I think someone else has been here today," I said, pointing to a blanket and picnic basket near the tree. "And what is that?" I pointed to what looked like a round table covered with a tarp.

"More of your surprise, m'lady. I was here and set this up this afternoon."

He helped me to slide off Snowball, caught me and kissed me before my feet could touch the ground. He tied Snowball where he could graze on the tall grass and drink from the creek. Then he led me through the grass to the blanket. I opened the picnic basket and found bread, cheese, apples, grapes, cold chicken, deviled eggs and dark chocolate candies. He even brought carrots for Snowball. "Oh, Devlin, a feast! But, no wine?"

"Fear not, sweet Chloe," he told me and walked to the edge of the creek. He reached into the cold water and pulled out two bottles of White Water. "There is a corkscrew and two glasses in the picnic basket." He brought one bottle to the blanket, putting the second one back into the creek to keep it cold. "Natural refrigeration."

I found the corkscrew. He opened the bottle and poured us each a glass of the wine that tasted like liquid summer. We clinked glasses and drank. "When I am 100 years old, and reflect on the high points of my life, this day will stand out in my memory as one of the best. This whole summer has been wonderful." I sighed, trying not to think that this might be the end of our summer, trying not to wonder what was ahead for us, how we could keep up this long distance romance through the fall and winter.

I pulled the grapes out of the basket and I dropped a few into my wine. "Want some?" I asked. Devlin nodded and I dropped grapes into his glass also. If you've never tried this, you should. After drinking the wine, eat the wine-soaked grapes. Wonderful!

Devlin was leaning back on the blanket watching me. He always seemed to know what I was thinking. "It has been a wonderful summer for me too, Chloe, and it's not going to change just because summer's ending. I've got something to tell you. Dad and Tommy want to form a partnership between Wild River and Northern Lights."

I sat up, nearly spilling my wine. "A partnership," I repeated.

Devlin nodded. "It was *Chloe Sparkles* that gave them the idea. Blending some of our syrah grapes with the Old Mission pinot gris and chardonnay grapes gave it a special, unusual flavor that's been very successful. They want to develop some new blends, especially more New York/Michigan blends, and want me to work on them for both places. I'll be able to split my time between here and there."

"Oh, Devlin, that's wonderful. If you'll be in Traverse City more often and longer, we can spend more time together there even when we're both working."

"Yes, but wait, there's more. What would you think about being the retail manager at both locations? You'd have more staff, of course. You wouldn't be able to put in the long hours at Northern Light like you have been because you'd be here half of your time - with me."

"We'd have the same schedule, go back and forth together? Yes, yes, yes! That would be wonderful! When do we start? Is this okay with Jillian and Jackie?"

"Right now and yes. In fact, it was Jillian who first suggested it and Mom loves the idea. She's hoping that she and Dad can do more traveling. I didn't want to say anything to you too soon, but it's going to happen right away, with this harvest. We're partners and Tommy and Dad are letting me buy in – 25% ownership in the company."

"Oh, my God! This surprise just keeps getting better and better." I tackled him and kissed him, pinning him to the blanket.

"Did I mention you're getting a big raise?"

I laughed, "I'd do it for half the pay, just to be with you!" And I kissed him again. "Let's celebrate!" I ran my hands under his shirt, nipping at his earlobes with my teeth.

"Wait, wait, wait – you don't want the extra money?" Devlin was laughing at me.

"Okay, if you insist, I'll take it. Now get these clothes off so I can show you how happy I am." I ripped at the buttons on his denim shirt with one hand and tried to undo his belt with the other.

"Don't you want to eat first," Devlin said teasing me. I grabbed a deviled egg and mashed it into his mouth.

"There you go, now get naked!" I pulled my polo shirt off over my head. The warm sun felt good on my shoulders and Devlin felt good

163

under my hands. He unhooked my bra and I flung it aside, loving the feel of the soft breeze on my skin. Devlin's shirt followed my bra and our jeans went next.

Devlin kissed me deeply. Good thing I like deviled eggs. I'll never eat another one without remembering this day.

I felt wild and primitive making love in the meadow by the creek under the late summer afternoon sun. We had no fear of discovery. Devlin had been coming to this clearing for years and had never seen another person here. Snowball was contentedly grazing on the grass and paid no attention to our wanton activities. We could be as loud and as crazy as we wanted. And we were loud and crazy. Crazy in love and crazy happy.

* * *

Chapter 24

PRINCESS CLOTHILDE AND

SENOR DIABLO

Chloe

"Devlin?"

"Hmmmm…"

We were lying naked on the blanket, feeding each other cold chicken, cheese, and grapes. We needed nourishment - and wine.

"What's under that tarp? Is there more to this surprise?"

"Oh, I almost forgot."

"What is it?"

"Well, I heard that there was something you always wanted to do, but Tommy wouldn't let you. So, I set this up for you." He stood up and made a courtly bow to me, which looked kind of silly considering that he was stark naked. "Your wish is my command, Princess!"

It couldn't be! Could it? I looked at Devlin. He lifted his head and grinned at me. I got up from the blanket and ran to the tarp-covered table. I pulled off the tarp. It wasn't a table. It was an old wooden vat and it was more than half filled with beautiful, dusky, sun-warmed, juice-filled, deep purple grapes!

Devlin was behind me, arms around me. "Princess Clothilde, will you do me the honor of crushing the grapes with me?" he asked in a really awful Spanish accent.

I turned in his arms, pressing myself full length against his body, skin to skin, heart to heart. "Senor Diablo, it would be my pleasure to crush the grapes with you."

Devlin lifted me over the edge of the vat and set me gently into the grapes before vaulting over the edge and joining me. We both laughed at the feel of the warm grapes bursting under us. Soon we were slippery with the juice and struggling to keep hold of each other.

"I didn't try this before I wrote about it. It's harder than I thought," Devlin said, almost slipping under the mashed grapes as he drank dark purple juice from my belly button. Needless to say, neither one of us could be on top or the other would have drowned in the mess, but we found ways "to infuse the grapes with the flavor of our passion."

Laughing, sputtering, covered head to toe with sweet, sticky, mashed purple grapes, we fed on each other and on the grapes. It was the most fun I'd ever had. Daylight was fading and the mashed grapes were cooling. Devlin scooped up a handful of juice and drank it. I licked his fingers tasting the sweetness. "Tastes like grape jelly," I told him.

"That's 'cause these grapes are mostly concords. I hope you don't mind that I didn't use the cabernet grapes."

"This is the most incredibly romantic thing anyone has ever done for me. You could have used wild grapes from the woods. It wouldn't have mattered." I kissed him deeply. "Yum! Sweet wine isn't my favorite, but I sure do like this."

"Ummm, me too. If I make wine from these grapes, will you drink it with me on our wedding night?"

I looked at him, surprised once again. "Chloe," he said, struggling in the slippery grapes to get down on his knees, "Will you please marry me. I want you to be my wife; I want to be your husband. I will love you forever."

I was crying, tears of joy mixing with the grape juice on my cheeks. "Yes, yes, yes. I will marry you! I love you and want to be with you forever."

"Forever," Devlin repeated. "I may have to make cases of wine from these grapes to save until our 50th anniversary. I may need some help satisfying my sexy old wife then."

I laughed and splashed him with the juice. "I can't imagine what you'll be like in 50 years, but I'm sure I'll still love you."

He kissed me again. "I was hoping you'd say yes. I can't give you a crown with rubies and emeralds but I have a ring for you. It's over there in the pocket of my jeans."

I didn't wait for Devlin to help me out of the vat. I was out and running back to our clothes while he was still climbing out after me. He caught up with me as I found his jeans and he wrapped the blanket around my shoulders. "Here, you're going to get chilled."

He took his jeans from me, reached into the right front pocket and then reached into the left front pocket, then tried the back pockets, then the watch pocket, then both front pockets again. "It must have fallen out when I pulled them off." He dropped the jeans and started combing through the matted grass where we had been picnicking and frolicking. "There are flashlights in the saddlebags." He stood up and ran over to Snowball while I kept searching.

I spotted the sparkle of the diamonds in the flashlight beam. Devlin picked it up and knelt, naked and covered in mashed grape mess, and said solemnly, "Chloe, will you please marry me?"

"Yes," I said and he slipped the ring onto my left hand ring finger. It slid easily onto my slippery skin. Devlin shone the flashlight beam on my hand so I could get a good look. "It's beautiful!" And I kissed him again, closing my fingers into a fist so the ring could not slip off.

"There's just one problem," I said to Devlin as we were trying to wipe each other off with the blanket and find our clothes.

"Problem? I thought I thought of everything. What problem?"

"What are we going to tell our kids when they ask us how you proposed to me?"

Devlin laughed and hugged me. "I grew up hearing the Woodstock story, I think we can come up with a good story for the kids without going into too many details. But you have another problem."

"What?"

Devlin shone the light up into the tree. "There it is!" I said spotting my missing bra hanging from a branch too high for me to reach. "Can you get it down?"

Devlin shook his head. "It's staying right there! Someday when we bring our kids here for picnics, we can show them and tell them the story."

So I pulled on my polo shirt without the bra. We packed up the remains of the food and the empty wine bottles and climbed back on Snowball. Devlin knew a shortcut back to his barn and Snowball had no problem navigating his way through the woods in the moonlight.

Devlin's arms were around me and I was blissfully happy, sticky and tired, but blissfully happy. Tonight we would ride the white horse back through the forest to Devlin's house, our snug castle in the vineyards, shower off the rest of the grapes, sleep in each other's arms, and tomorrow we would start the beginning of our Happily Ever After.

I remembered Mrs. Montgomery telling me that the end of the fairy tale was just the beginning of real life. Tonight my handsome hero on the white horse had whisked me off to our romantic glade in the magic forest, made love to me in the grapes in the moonlight, and brought all of my fantasy fairy tales to life.

Now I was looking forward to the rest of the story. If Happily Ever After was just the beginning, it was a hell of a beginning and I was going to enjoy every moment of what was to come.

* * *

The end – or just the beginning…

16741138R00100

Made in the USA
Charleston, SC
08 January 2013